MINIONS OF MARS

MINIONS OF MARS

WILLIAM GRAY BEYER

COVER ILLUSTRATION BY

VIRGIL FINLAY

STEEGER BOOKS • 2019

PUBLISHING HISTORY

"Minions of Mars" originally appeared in the January 13, 20, 27, February 3, and 10, 1940 issues of *Argosy* magazine (Vol. 296, Nos. 2–6). Copyright © 1940 by The Frank A. Munsey Company. Copyright renewed © 1967 and assigned to Steeger Properties, LLC. All rights reserved.

Visit steegerbooks.com for more books like this.

FOREWORD

MARK NEVIN, AWAY back in the twentieth century A.D., had a stomach ache. Then his doctor diagnosed his ailment as appendicitis and persuaded Mark to be the first to try his new anaesthetic. Something slipped, and Mark slept peacefully on in a blissful state of suspended animation.

While Mark was napping, a cataclysmic war broke out that shattered civilization.

Things were a little better when Mark finally did come to, but he might have fared badly just the same but for the intervention of one Omega, a disembodied intelligence.

He selects Mark to be the father of the neo-man and chooses the lovely Nona as his mate, which is agreeable as Mark has already fallen in love with her. He imparts a radioactive element to their blood.

With Mark as leader, Omega enlists an army of Vikings to wipe out two malignant intelligences which threaten to destroy the world. Victorious, the Vikings, Mark and Nona take their leave of Omega and sail for home.

CHAPTER I

HAIL FELLOW

A LONE FIGURE stood atop the little knoll and gazed in perplexity at the distant city. Eyes shaded from the glaring light

of the rising sun he seemed to be seeing a sight beyond under-standing. He turned back and as he did so, the golden light of the sun caught the play of powerful muscles under his bronzed skin. Brief leather trunks, as pliable and almost as close-fitting as his own skin, were held by a broad belt from which hung a shiny hand-axe. He wore no other clothing except a helmet, adorned with wings and considerably battered.

His face was as strong as his smoothly muscled body. The clear, blue eyes were baffled, haunted by a persistently elusive memory. He seemed to have forgotten everything he ever knew. It had taken him, for instance, more than a day to remember his own name. It had only come to him a few hours ago. Mark Nevin. And now, as his hand brushed the axe in turning, he caught the fleeting recollection that he had been known as Mark the Axe-thrower. The axe-thrower—idiotic! But of course there was the axe—but whom did he throw it at—and why?

Experimentally, he drew the axe and let fly at, a sapling fifty yards away. It was a tremendous throw, but he didn't know that. Nor was he much surprised when the axe sped true and sheared

through the four-inch tree. His only emotion, as he retrieved the weapon, was a certain satisfaction that he had earned his name. Mark, the Axe-thrower, it was. Whatever that meant.

Briefly he inspected the axe before returning it to his belt. There was something he should remember about it; something he couldn't quite grasp. The weapon was a solid piece of metal. Its entire surface was gleaming with a tarnish-proof luster. Stainless steel, he would have called it if he could have remembered the term. But he couldn't.

There was some association here, but no amount of concentration would bring it to the fore. Only the dim thought struggled to the surface, that here was a thing of great antiquity. And he wondered how he knew that. For the axe was as shiny as one made and polished an hour ago. One thing he did know, and that was that he must not distrust these vague recollections of his. There was a lot to remember, and he had the uncomfortable feeling that someone, somewhere, depended on him to remember.

HE COULD see that someone and he knew her name. She

had been with him since his first conscious memory yesterday morning. The vision of her loveliness had been with him in the salty water as he swam toward the land he was now exploring. Even then he had known her name—Nona.

But no amount of thinking had brought the slightest added knowledge. It was very irritating to recall her so perfectly, and not actually to know the slightest thing about her.

Discontentedly, he turned and faced the distant city. There he would find human beings. And it was most likely that among humans he would find the thought associations that would stir his tantalizing memory.

There were no workers in the tilled fields about the city. Nor any movement in the harbor on his left. The sun made long shadows of the masts of these vessels, and the rippling of the waves turned the shadows into writhing snakes. But there was no other motion.

There was an explanation for this gloomy quiet, and a simple one at that. It was still early, and the inhabitants of the city were simply still in bed. But even if this simple fact had been explained to him, he would have found it strange. For Mark was not the same as other men in this respect. He didn't waste the sun-less hours of the night in stupor. He was as active then as he was in the daytime.

Mark was not even aware that normal men needed sleep and food. For in the short day and night of his conscious existence he had done none of these things, and had felt no loss. He was a self-sufficient machine, and he felt marvelously fit and vigorous as he strode rapidly toward the city.

Mark, with the childlike trust of the innocent or the not-quite-bright, made no attempt to be stealthy.

He was walking beside a broad, cobbled path. This was an ox-cart road, he recognized, and then wondered how he knew. There were no ox-carts to be seen. And certainly in the day and night of his memory he had seen no such conveyances, nor the roads on which they traveled.

Somewhere beyond that day and night such things must have been familiar.

The sight of the cobbles seemed to touch some familiar chord, and experimentally he stepped on them. They were uncomfortable to his bare feet, and he moved back to the smooth dirt by the side of the road. Then the struggling memory came to the surface.

It was the smooth feel of the caked dirt which carried the association. For an instant he seemed to see a road stretching endlessly into the distance. Rushing along its hard, smooth surface were wheeled vehicles, traveling at breakneck speed.

The vision passed, and with its passing came the realization that the road he had seen and the automobiles moving on it, were things of antiquity equal to that of his axe. Such things no longer existed, he was acutely aware. And yet he felt that even with the knowledge that thousands of years had gone since their existence, nevertheless he had seen such roads and traveled in such cars. This was getting more unnerving at every second, and he decided that unless he could remember everything at once, it would be more comfortable not to remember anything at all.

The cobbled road led directly between two buildings at the edge of the city. It continued as a street, narrow and shadowy. Mark walked on, intent on finding men. And men he found, though not quite in the way he had expected. He had gone perhaps a half-mile, when abruptly a horde of yelling maniacs catapulted from an alley and bore him to the ground!

THERE HAD been no warning, and the thing was so sudden that he hadn't had time even to let out a yip of protest. Then he was lying wonderingly beneath a ton or so of evil smelling humanity and waiting patiently for further developments. He felt no more resentment, than he had felt pain from the beating he had taken.

His assailants were more surprised than he. Surely, thought they, a man of such tremendous physique would require mighty strenuous subduing. Disappointed and a little relieved, too, they lifted themselves off their prisoner's body. Two of them eased their feelings by cuffing him as they rose. The blows, while vigorous, caused only a momentary twinge and Mark blissfully ignored them. He was busy watching the astonished expressions on their faces, as he sprang, unmarked and, unhurt, to his feet.

This was not a new experience, he realized, noticing that several of his attackers were holding short clubs in their hands. Sometime in the past men had attacked him with weapons and had been surprised that he had emerged unscathed. For the first time he sensed the fact that he was in some manner different from other men. That for some unaccountable reason he was hardier and less easily damaged. This, he decided, was probably a good thing.

"Hooray?" suddenly demanded the foremost of his captors. "Mac or Mic?"

Mark frowned momentarily. Then he grinned. For into his continually astonishing brain had popped the knowledge that a Mac was a Scotchman and a Mic, an Irishman.

"Yank," he answered, and then wondered why he said it. In his head came the sound of a baseball popping off a bat, although Mark didn't realize what it was.

"No such!" declared the other. "Soo!"

Whereupon his attackers closed in fore and aft, and marched him down the street, clubs held menacingly. Mark was still grinning as he walked between them. He wanted to go into the city anyway.

His eyes fell on the leader of the crowd and he was surprised to note that the beefy one was carrying his axe. He hadn't known he had lost it, but realized that it had probably been wrenched from his belt during the short scuffle. Somehow the axe didn't seem a dangerous weapon in the leader's possession. He wondered if he was also immune from damage by axecuts. It annoyed him that he couldn't remember why he was different from normal humans.

Right now he resolved not to let the axe get out of his sight.

He knew that somehow it was connected with the past, and that he mustn't lose it.

Here and there as they marched, a sleepy-looking head would poke out of a window to see what the night-watch had caught. Mark grinned at them, one and all, and usually got a startled look in reply. His captors were very military in their manner, assiduously keeping in step. They were burly and dressed in ill-fitting uniforms of coarse cloth, and armed with daggers which were fastened in their belts, in addition to the short clubs.

Mark with his vast splotches of ignorance, could not, of course, know that it was not exactly military in the most rigorous tradition for the guards to chatter like monkeys as they marched. Some of the words and expressions they used were unfamiliar ones, but most of their conversation Mark was able to translate into intelligible meaning. This puzzled him for a while, but as their words became more understandable he forgot about it. They were talking English, he knew, and the reason it sounded strange was probably that they spoke a dialect he had never heard. It didn't occur to him that he was listening to English as it was spoken several thousand years after he had learned the language as a boy.

The conversation centered about him. Guesses were being made as to what manner of man he might be; and why he hadn't suffered from the cudgel blows they had administered; and finally as to what disposition might be made of him by the local magistrate. Quite a few guesses were made concerning the last, and they varied all the way from slavery in the fields to burning at the stake. One fellow, on Mark's left, voiced the opinion that the proper punishment for his crime of breaking curfew, should be a term in the king's army.

"That's no punishment!" exclaimed the man next to him, although he didn't say it in quite that way. "The army lives high."

"I know it," replied the other, complacently. "But when I tell the magistrate what I saw, that's what he'll say, too."

"What did you see?"

The first man carefully drew forth his knife. Mark noticed that it was stained with a bluish streak along its cutting edge. The stain seemed to sparkle with an iridescent sheen. The second guardsman looked at it stupidly.

"That's where I sliced him on the shoulder," explained the first man. "Look at the shoulder. The left one."

MORE CURIOUS than they, Mark twisted his head to look at it too. There was a smear of the same bluish substance, but no cut. It had healed in such a short time that only a teaspoonful of blood had been spilled. One of the watchmen was also looking at the smear spot, his face portraying a certain amount of awe intermingled with profound respect.

"It's only a scratch," he murmured. "What bothers me is that blue stuff. You don't suppose he bleeds *blue*, do you?"

"It was no scratch," his friend insisted. "You know I always take a good slash when the sergeant isn't looking. Now wouldn't this lad make a soldier?"

The other shrugged. "Blue," he muttered, unhappily. "Gorm."

Mark's brow was creased in a deep frown. Dimly he was grasping another section of his vanished past. Blood, he knew, should be red, not an iridescent blue. And this blood of his, which refused to follow the rules, had something to do with his differing from normal mortals. Was he really the freak these idiots seemed to think him?

He hardly noticed when they turned into a large courtyard, and stopped before a huge door of oak, studded and banded with iron. The sergeant hammered on it with his club, while the rest of them relaxed as if they expected a long wait.

Mark's mind was going like blazes. Because he was remembering. Remembering a period of intense pain. He was remembering also the serious face of old Doc Kelso, who wanted his permission to use his new anaesthetic in the performance of the appendectomy he must undergo. It was all coming back....

Abruptly he was snapped to the present. A club-blow between the shoulder blades almost knocked him down. He caught himself, however, and spun round in fury. Blast them, just as it was all coming back, too. He stopped short at the sight of a dozen drawn daggers. Perhaps it wouldn't be smart to test the peculiar power of his blood against so many of those knives. After all, why become hash merely because of overconfidence? And in that moment of hesitation he was forced through the now open portal.

Mark caught a fleeting glimpse of a small room with a table at which were seated three soldiers playing cards. A fourth was swinging open another massive door of oak. Mark was given a shove through this one also. A short, dark corridor led them past a series of barred doors, from behind which Mark heard a variety of snores, all in different keys. Before he had a chance to wonder where he was being led, he found himself thrust forcibly into an unoccupied cell.

The door clanged shut and the sound of retreating footsteps mingled with the nasal serenade.

CHAPTER II

FOOTPRINTS IN TIME

IN THE COURSE of the world's history there have been many methods of propulsion through water. Fish have used fins and tails almost since time began. Squid-like creatures utilize rocket propulsion, by swelling a muscle-lined bladder with water and then squeezing it out again. Man's earliest attempts involved the use of both hands and feet in swimming. A more advanced effort consisted of lying prone on a short log and paddling with the hands. Then some inspired genius hit upon the idea of hollowing out the log and paddling with shaped paddles.

From this crude beginning the evolution of boats probably has paralleled very closely the cultural advance of the race. For with the improvement in boats came an interchange of ideas between groups far removed from each other. Thus it was that when man had attained his highest cultural status during the waning years of the twentieth century, travel over and through water had also reached its peak of efficiency.

But when the peoples of the world decided to war upon one another, as these boats were the ultimate in transportation, so was this war the ultimate in destruction. Thus it was that with the end of the war man found himself cast back almost to the point when he was propelling a dugout with a paddle.

That was the last war for many a year; it was so completely destructive, so devastating, that when it had at last burnt itself out, man had sunk to such low estate that he could think of nothing to fight about except the immediate necessities of life.

But ships, ever the measuring-rod of man's progress, had again started their slow evolution toward the ultimate perfection they must some day regain. And the culture of man was keeping step.

The first morning rays of a golden sun caught the upper portion of a huge, sagging square-sail, and touched it with fire. A man from the tenth century would have found the ship to have some familiar characteristics, but only a person living in the eightieth century would have recognized it for what it was. A vessel of the north-country sea-rovers—peopled by yellow-haired giants who would rather do battle than eat—and who had prodigious appetites.

The ship was becalmed, and this was a vessel which need never be becalmed. Its sides were lined with a single row of long oars, now cocked at an angle, so that the blades were well out of the water. The rigging of the sail, which was far more scientific and manageable than any used by tenth-century Vikings, allowed it to make use of the slightest current of air, and in any direction except straight ahead.

APATHY REIGNED among the voyagers on this ship. No definite course of action had been decided upon. A difference of opinion existed concerning whether they should return to their home port or continue the fruitless search that had occupied them for the past day and night. There was the urge to keep searching but in each was the knowledge that it was futile. For no man could swim in the open sea for a day and a night.

Leaning against a short section of rail, and gazing with tragic eyes out over the waves, stood a young woman, beautiful even in her grief. The yellow-haired Norsemen, sprawled wearily about on the deck, glanced occasionally at her, and then quickly looked elsewhere. It was her man who had been lost, but they were able to feel her grief almost as acutely as she. For the lost man was Mark, the Axe-thrower, favored of Thor, and the personal hero of every man on board.

Nona's lovely body reflected the weariness she endured as she left the rail and made for her cabin. But hers was only a fatigue of mind, manifesting itself in a body that was really tireless. Her blood was charged with the same cell-renewing element that made Mark the perfect physical machine that he was. But so grueling had been the waiting and hoping that she imagined fatigue where no fatigue could be. Wearily she slumped into a soft chair. Hope had fled, and there remained only a numbing, tearless grief.

Then abruptly she sprang to her feet, one hand stifling an involuntary scream. Across the room, squatting in a corner, was a creature that would have raised terror in the stoutest of humans.

Superficially the thing was an enormous spider, fully two feet across the body. Superficially, insofar as it possessed eight legs attached to its bulbous cephalothorax. But different, in that it had six tentacles, three on a side, on its upper surface.

Each of these members was about three feet long and was divided at the end into two flexible prehensile fingers. And different also, by reason of the segmented, chitinous armor which covered the body. But, spider or no spider, the thing was a witch's fancy, the hideous product of a creator gone mad. Nona thought perhaps she ought to scream anyway. So she did.

"Calm yourself, girl," came a voice from the general direction of the creature. "It's only me... Omega. I just wanted to see how

a human would react to the sight of one of the former inhabitants of the moon. This was my original body, you know. I assume
you're not exactly in favor of it?"

Nona slumped again into the chair. "Oh, it's you," she said
irritably. "Don't you know this isn't any time for your silly tricks?"
She winced at the sight of him.

"And whatever that thing is you're wearing, please destroy it."

"It was destroyed more than five hundred centuries ago," said
the voice. "You know that. You might call this thing an astral
projection—it's been dead so long. But really it's only a figment
of *your* imagination."

"It's certainly no figment of *my* imagination, you celestial
prankster. No self-respecting girl would ever work up a thing
like that."

"You certainly did imagine it," Omega snapped pettishly.
"I made you. And I'm not very pleased at the way you react to
my natural body. I considered it quite handsome at one time.
But then, I might have felt the same way about yours when I
was young. But I've seen so many forms of life in the last five
hundred centuries that they all seem natural to me now...."

While he talked, Omega caused the vision of the spider-like
creature to vanish, and in its stead Nona saw the bent figure of
an aged, bearded man. At the sight of this senile being she closed
her eyes and relaxed. Then she burst our crying. Omega cocked
a sympathetic eye at her. He hated weepy women, but if Nona
had stooped to tears, there was a reason. "Nona, what's wrong?"
he queried, gently.

"Mark..." She choked as she tried to tell him. "He's... he's
dead!"

"Dead! What's he mean, the young loafer? He knows he can't
die—it would upset all my plans. I'll show him! Where's the
body? I'll bring him back...."

He stopped short as Nona, still sobbing, waved an arm toward
the two portholes at the side of the cabin. Through them he

could see the sunlit waves of the North Sea. Then, surprisingly, he chuckled.

"Fell overboard, eh?" He chuckled again, Nona looked at him in astonishment. "That's all right then. Now start at the beginning and tell me what happened."

NONA'S EYES widened in sudden hope, for Omega was something close to omnipotent to her, and if he said that Mark might not be dead....

Abruptly she broke into speech, nearly incoherent at first, but getting clearer as hope calmed her nerves. She told of the storm which had come up during their trip to Stadtland, on the coast of Norway; of how the wind had driven the ship toward the south and west, far off its course.

Mark had made her keep to the cabin, and when he was lost she had known nothing of it until the storm had abated. Sven, the captain, had broken the news to her in the morning, and since then the ship had been searching, fruitlessly.

"Well, what are you worrying about?" demanded Omega, his wrinkled face beaming with an impish grin.

"He... Can't he drown?"

"Of course not. Drowning is suffocation, And how can a man who doesn't need air suffocate?"

"But Mark and I both breathe. And if I try to stop, my lungs go to work as soon as I stop thinking about it. I suppose it's the same with him."

"Of course," Omega agreed. "But that is only because there is a nerve center in your brain which controls such involuntary actions. The fluid which I injected into your veins didn't stop that from working, but it did remove the necessity of having a constant supply of oxygen. Therefore Mark's respiration would continue normally, but it wouldn't matter to him whether he was breathing air or water, or strawberry jam. He doesn't require oxygen for the function of his body.

"I told you once that your body and Mark's are burning the power from the radioactive element in your blood. You need no other fuel to keep you alive. No food and consequently no oxygen to support the combustion of that food. All you require is water, and Mark is getting plenty of that. Yes, indeed, I imagine he's getting enough water to last him a lifetime." He grinned happily.

"But it is sea water," objected Nona. "Wouldn't that…."

"No—it wouldn't," Omega said, impatiently. "I can't explain the exact nature of your present body chemistry. You couldn't understand it. But you know very well that you have lived without eating since I gave you that injection several months ago. So you should be willing to take my word that sea water is as safe for Mark as spring water."

Nona was smiling quietly now. Where another woman might have let herself go into hysterics from reaction, Nona's temperament forbade such a weakness. Normally calm and placid, she was busily telling herself that she had known it all the time. That Mark couldn't be dead. Only the grueling hours of constant searching could have made her temporarily lose hope. But even so she wanted to hear more assurance from Omega.

"It's October," she pointed out. "Cold and exhaustion…."

"Nonsense! Mark can't become exhausted. Not for several thousand years to come, anyhow. Radioactivity supplies his energy, more than he can use by muscular activity. He could swim the Atlantic without tiring! And as for cold…." Here Omega hesitated. "Take a look in that mirror." He leered at her unnervingly.

Nona obediently crossed the cabin to a highly ornamented full-length mirror, Her reflection showed a beautifully formed body, which womanlike, she briefly admired, even lifting a hand to tuck away a stray, ebon curl. She noted, too, the trimness of her attire. A short jacket of satiny material, which came as low as her lower ribs; then an expanse of tanned skin, beneath which was a loose-fitting pair of shorts of the same shiny cloth. But that was what all the women wore in the summer. The only difference was in the colors and—

"I see it's dawned on you," said Omega. "The temperature is somewhere near freezing. Even the tough lads out on the deck are better clothed than you."

"You mean that our blood protects Mark and me from cold?"

"Of course. You would have noticed it sooner or later, if I hadn't told you. Radioactivity doesn't depend on temperature, and as a result your sensory nerves aren't giving you any warning of discomfort because of the low temperature. Your chemistry operates with equal efficiency over a wide range of heat fluctuation."

"Then Mark is safe. But where is he?"

"How should I know? Suppose you go on deck and tell Sven to point the ship toward Norway. Tell him you've had a vision or something, and that you know that Mark is alive and will rejoin you, later. He worships Mark, and that will be a kindness. You can say that Thor himself has revealed that he has given Mark a mission to fulfill, and that he will return when he finishes.

"Sven will believe that a lot quicker than an explanation of the real facts. And in the meantime I shall go and find your missing husband. And keep your chin up. I dare say it's a very lovely one, although being a spider I wouldn't know."

There was a twinkle in Omega's aged eyes, to match the impish grin, when he abruptly vanished.

NONA SAT still for a moment, smiling toward the place which Omega had just quitted. Then she opened the cabin door and stepped out. A moment later a flock of sea gulls which had been perched in the rigging, took sudden wing, startled by the wild shouts of joy that were rising from the deck.

Yet if Omega had returned and told them of the thing he had just discovered, those shouts might have turned to groans. Omega, a disembodied intelligence of the first order, had been perfectly confident that he could touch Mark's mind at once.

Such a mental feat was a problem of simple accomplishment to one of his intellect. Fifty thousand years of projecting his mind to the far ends of the universe, had given him a

mind power not surpassed anywhere. His over-active curiosity concerning the myriad of life-forms that infest the endless
number of worlds in a dozen galaxies, kept him always alert
and always a dynamo of mental energy. And yet he couldn't
contact Mark!

The mind-pattern that was Mark, had temporarily ceased
to exist. For that mind pattern was not complete without all its
memories. If a disembodied intelligence can shudder, Omega
came very close to it. For in that instant, the thought came to
him that the only answer could be that he was dead, after all.

And Omega had become very attached to Mark.

In Mark and Nona he had pictured the means of populating
the earth with a type of human far superior to the product that
nature had blindly created. He had chosen them as Adam and
Eve for this race of the future because of the dominating good
in their characters. And now, it seemed, Mark had ceased to be.

But in the instant that this thought came into existence,
Omega's brilliant mind rejected it. There could be another reason
for his failure to contact the mindpattern that he knew as Mark.

Since their last intercourse, Mark might have changed. His
ideas, his fundamental philosophy of life might have altered for
some reason, and thus created a mindpattern that was unrecognizable. Omega rejected this also.

Only one alternative remained. Mark had been washed overboard. It was likely that he had received a sharp blow on the head
as he went over. If this had happened, then it was possible that
the blow could have damaged his brain. And the mindpattern
had changed as a consequence.

BUT THIS complicated things dreadfully. Concussion could
cause a partial or even complete loss of memory. Fracture might
do either, and in addition might result in irreparable damage to
the brain tissue. Mark may have changed only to the extent of
losing some of his memories, or he may have been reduced to a
hopeless idiot. Either way Omega *must* find him. For he alone
possessed the knowledge to restore him.

Not knowing the extent of the pattern change, Omega would have to mentally visualize a pattern containing Mark's present dominant characteristics. Then he would have to make contact with any being possessing that pattern. There was every chance that no living being would respond to such an imagined mind-pattern. And if one did, it would probably be the wrong man.

Yet it was the only way. He might have to project a million of them before he hit upon the proper one. But with an energy that was definitely not human, he set about the task.

For two days he labored mightily at his problem. He visualized patterns of the most simple structures, then advanced to others containing some of the memories that he knew were Mark's. Nothing resulted.

Exasperated, he went back again to the more simple patterns, thinking he might have failed to imagine some little detail. Then ahead again to more complicated ones.

Omega knew all about Mark. He had delved into the innermost recesses of Mark's memory until the mind and character of Mark were as familiar as his own. Each pattern he was forming contained more memories than the last. He had reached the point in the memory chain where Mark had met Nona, when he suddenly realized that he couldn't hope to succeed by the present method.

There was one pesky thing he had forgotten. And that was that Mark, wherever he was, now had some new memories of which he knew nothing. Since the time he had fallen overboard Mark had been experiencing things that Omega couldn't know about. This, of course, wouldn't make any difference ordinarily. Omega could always contact a familiar mind-pattern, even though years of time had passed and new experiences had partially changed its former structure. But that was because the new memories were only a small portion of the total memories of the pattern. In the present case the new memories would constitute almost, the entire pattern.

But there was another way. And though Omega cringed

mentally at the thought of trying it, he knew very well it was the only course he could take. The method lay in an ability he had discovered shortly after he and the other members of his dying race had cast off their bodies and had taken residence in the imperishable brain containers which now rested on a dead and airless moon. He, differing from his compatriots, hadn't been satisfied to stay there, whiling away the ages in abstract thought. His ego had ventured away from the brain which had given it birth, and he had gone forth to explore the universe.

He could think himself instantly to the far corners of the universe. He could construct and inhabit any sort of body he wished. And he had full control and use of the vast stores of energy which are everywhere in space.

And then, almost accidentally, Omega had discovered that he could travel about in time, as well.

He had tried it, gingerly at first, and found that there were decided limitations. He could observe past happenings but could take no part in them. He couldn't take a body and mingle with the beings he was interested in, because he hadn't really been there when the things had happened. Nor could he force himself backward in time beyond the date of his own birth.

That fact had handicapped him, for he was young then, and therefore, couldn't go back very far into the history of any race he might be studying. But as far as it went, the ability had its uses.

But he had come to grief when he had tried to clear up a hazy point in the past of his own race. The event which he had wanted to watch had taken place within his own lifetime, and, in fact, was connected with some of his own past operations. The trouble came when he had run across his own former body in the course of his study.

The two identities, being so near alike, had merged! He had been forced to live his lifetime all over again, up to the point where he again existed as a bodiless entity. That had been a great nuisance and a hideous waste of time.

The experience had taught him an extreme caution in connection with this special ability. True, he had used it again a few times, when his curiosity had overcome his caution, but each time he had been half frightened to death for fear he might run into himself again.

And now, after thousands of years of aimless perambulating, the thought of having to repeat himself over again gave him a disembodied fit of ague.

He would, however, try it once again.

This process was, if anything, a longer one than the business of trying to match mind patterns. It was a simple thing to place himself in the position the ship had occupied during the storm. And he had the satisfaction of observing Mark's head strike the ship's rail a glancing blow as he was washed over. That would teach him to be more careful.

The fact that Mark almost immediately began to strike out in a firm, distance covering stroke, proved that he was not greatly damaged. But the fact that he didn't once look around for the ship and try to reach it, also proved that he had no memory of it.

In the few moments from the time his head struck the rail until he began to swim, he had regained consciousness, devoid of memory!

And here began Omega's troubles. He couldn't speed up the course of events which had happened and were unchangeable. He couldn't observe them at high speed as one would a moving picture of the same events. He had to watch them as they happened.

Until Mark had found some spot where Omega could be reasonably sure that he would stay for a few days, he didn't dare jump back to the present and start a search for him. Mark might in the interim have moved to a distant point.

Then, just when Omega was satisfied that Mark would very likely remain for a few days in Scarbor, inasmuch as he had followed him as far as the edge of the city and witnessed his capture, events started happening which made him decide he had better watch for a while longer.

CHAPTER III

IRON BARS DO NOT
A PRISON MAKE

MARK GAZED AROUND the gloomy interior of his cell. It was devoid of furniture, though it wasn't entirely unadorned. In one corner there was a contraption of chains and manacles fastened to the wall. On the floor underneath was a pile of human bones and a jawless skull. Mark gulped. "Hello," he said to the skull. "Fine day." But the skull only grinned, with a knowing look to its empty sockets.

Whenever Mark straightened up, he banged his head on the ceiling. The cell had a foul smell, too. Altogether he was disinclined to stay for any great length of time. His eyes returned to the skull, he leaned over, picked it up, and looked absently into the eyeless sockets. They seemed to look back at him with a prophetic expression. He hastily returned the thing to its place on the top of the heap. No, he wasn't going to like this place.

Mark crouched on the chilly floor and tried to remember more about himself.

He didn't succeed very well, because every time he was on the track of something, the vision of the lovely lady intruded. And every time he saw her, she became clearer and more desirable, until she was like an ache in his heart.

Little memories came back.

Once he saw her breaking twigs and arranging them as if to build a fire. Again she would be swinging along at his side, as they made their way through a dense wood.... That woman who was so desirable, was his! There was no doubt of it now. And he must find her. Somewhere in the confused past lay the clue that would lead to her. He must remember!

He sank deep in thought.

As the morning sun rose higher in the sky, it became lighter in the cell. Mark was startled out of his reverie by the sight of another row of cells, on the opposite side of the corridor. The one directly across from his contained an unkempt individual who was leaning against the bars of the cell door, regarding Mark with a, quizzical expression. A fiery shock of red hair threatened to cut off his vision, although he evidently could see through it, for he grinned when he realized that Mark saw him.

MARK GRINNED back. He thought he should say something, but couldn't think of anything. Red-head broke the silence. "A new customer," he observed. "What are you in for?"

This one spoke in a new dialect, but Mark translated it automatically into the English of his youth.

"I don't know," Mark confessed. "They just grabbed me and hauled me in."

"Didn't they beat you up?"

"No, just a few blows with their clubs."

"You're lucky. You must have broke curfew, and they usually jump a curfew breaker and beat him up before he knows what's happening."

"Why?"

"Serious offense," explained the other. "They're all so scary in this place that they pass laws to keep everybody off the streets after dark. The only ones who break curfew are thieves and murderers. And the night-watch always beats them up—when they catch them."

"I see… But they didn't catch me after dark. The sun had been up for quite a while."

"It's still curfew time now," informed the red-head. "The gong rings at about eight at night, and then it doesn't ring in the morning until about seven. There it goes now!"

A deep-throated chime filled the air of the cell-room with its throbbing vibration.

"I'm Murf," volunteered the red-head. "What's your name?"

"Mark."

The sound of the gongs had awakened other inmates of the prison.

In the cell next to Mark's a man called to Murf. He spoke in a clipped accent, and rolled his r's. Mark decided he was a Scot, known here as a Mac.

"Have you thought of anything?" he inquired.

"No, Oateater, but I will," said Murf.

"And what'll ye use to do it with?" retorted the Scotchman. Then he laughed heartily. "That last one you tried will go down in history. You might not have been sick when you pretended to be, but you surely were afterward. What with the flogging, and all." He laughed again, and Mark wondered vaguely if there was something the matter with his sense of humor too. But Murf wasn't laughing either.

"It would have worked," maintained Murf, "if the man had been carrying the keys."

"You were too busy having a convulsion to look."

"All right. All right. Have a good laugh. But when I do get a good scheme, don't expect me to waste time opening your door."

This quieted the Scot. Mark wasn't sure what was meant by their conversation, and he didn't get time to figure it out. His attention was distracted by an unholy clamor further down in the cell block. Men were rattling the cell doors and shouting for food.

PRESENTLY THE massive door from the courtyard swung open, admitting three men and a flat cart. Two of the men were obviously soldiers. They were armed with swords and daggers, and wore breastplates of lacquered armor. These were two of the four guardsmen he had seen briefly the night before. He was to learn later that these prison guards were soldiers in the service of the city constabulary forces. They were of a slightly higher order than the members of the night-watch, a separate branch of the same force. They were better armed and better paid. Besides their soft berth, as guardsmen, they were occasionally called out for duty in quelling civil disorders beyond the capacity of the night-watch.

The soldiers took positions at each side of the door while the third man pushed the cart to the center of the corridor, and distributed the wooden plates.

Mark received his ration and looked at it distastefully. Even if he had wanted food, he certainly wouldn't have wanted that mess.

"Murf," he called, his voice competing with a medley of eating sounds.

"Umph?" answered the red-head, chewing mightily.

"It just occurred to me that I'm guilty of the crime of breaking curfew, even though I never heard of it. What's the penalty?"

"Drawin' and quarterin'," replied Murf, swallowing a prodigious chunk of meat.

Drawing and quartering.

MARK NODDED. Then he realized that he didn't know what drawing and quartering was. He asked Murf. Murf tossed back his hair.

"Listen! I told you that curfew breakers were either thieves or murderers. Therefore they're treated as such. Drawn and quartered!"

"I heard you," Mark said. "But what is it?"

"Say, where did you come from? That's standard punishment all over."

"Oh," said Mark. "Is it?"

"You're a funny one," declared Murf, looking at him sharply. "But if you want to know—they nail you to a wall with spikes through your hands and feet. Then they stick a knife in your belly, reach in and grab one end of the mess that's in there, and draw it out slowly. That's the drawing part. It lasts for a while and you don't die right away if the fellow knows his job.

"You understand that? Well—

"Then they cut you in four. That's the quartering part. I'm

against it, myself. And there's only a slight chance of getting any
other sentence. Sometimes the magistrate gets a notion to vary
the monotony by having a man burned at the stake, or hung, but
it's usually drawin' and quarterin'."

"Sounds messy," was all Mark said.

The redhead went back to his meal with a relish. He finished,
wiped his mouth on a sleeve, and skimmed the wooden plate
in the direction of the big door. Mark had been inspecting the
rusted bars of his cell door, but looked up at the sound of the
clattering plate.

"Are you still hungry?"

"I'm always hungry," replied Murf.

Mark nodded and grasped two adjoining bars of the door. No
strain showed in his face, but the sinews of his arms stood out
like steel cables and the muscles of his shoulders knotted and
threatened to push through his bronzed skin. Slowly the two
bars bent. As they did so, the lower ends lifted out of the holes
in the bottom of the door.

No other man could have maintained that terrific pressure
even if he could have exerted it. But the radioactive element
which supplied Mark's energy was constant, and built up
broken-down cell tissue in an instant.

Eventually the bars bent so far that they were clear, and Mark
jerked them asunder with a savage wrench.

Then he bent over, picked up his plateful of garbage and
calmly stepped through the opening. He handed the dish to a
pop-eyed Murf. Murf took it, numbly.

"Look," he finally whispered, "I'm not so hungry now. Do you
suppose you could do that to my door?"

Mark nodded. "I don't see why not." It didn't take so long this
time, for he had noticed how the bars lifted through the holes.
He took his grip further down, and the job was accomplished
in half the time. Murf stepped through, the plate of food still
in his bands.

A sort of subdued bedlam arose when the other prisoners saw

what had happened. Each prisoner whispered his demand to be released, too. Mark had no intention of taking time to operate on any more cell doors. He was searching for an exit.

Abruptly the clamor ceased. Mark had found the window, but he turned to see what had happened. He saw Murf with his hands raised for quiet.

"It's broad daylight," he told them. "And if the whole gang breaks out, they'll nail us right away. But the two of us can make it. There won't be any trials until after the holidays, so you're safe for a while. If you'll swear allegiance to my cause, we'll come back on the first moonless night and turn you loose. What say?"

Another hushed murmur, not quite as loud as the last, and Murf darted down the corridor to join Mark. He looked up at the window, about nine feet off the floor. It also was barred. As if the two men had rehearsed the thing for months, they went into action.

Mark leaped for the bars, grasped them, and Murf moved against the wall, placing his shoulders under Mark's bare feet. Standing thus, Mark was able to exert pressure. It took a little longer, for the bars were fastened deeply into the stone of the jail wall.

It was a matter of several minutes before the two fugitives found themselves safely in an alleyway back of the jail. Murf was panting with excitement and exertion, and seemed anxious to get away from the immediate vicinity as quickly as possible. Impatiently he tugged at Mark's arm, muttering urgently, as he regained his breath.

"Calm yourself, friend," admonished Mark. "They don't even know we've escaped, as yet. But if we attract attention by hurrying too much…."

"You're a cool one," Murf said. "Who are you, anyway?"

"I don't really know," Mark admitted. "I've got to find out. That's why I couldn't stay in there any longer."

"Oh, sure. You wasn't worried about being kilt at all."

MURF GLANCED at the winged helmet, which Mark still

retained, and an expression of sly cunning crossed his face for the briefest instant.

Mark missed the look, for they had reached the end of the alley and he was inspecting the street before them. There were several pedestrians about, and one ox-cart was progressing slowly in their direction. Mark noticed that there seemed to be no uniformity of dress among those on the street.

There were a few women, apparently of the poorer class, and in the next block he could see two men who were probably soldiers. Across the street was a party of four men, partially intoxicated, whom he took to be sailors returning to their ship after a night of carousing. Except for the fact that all those in sight had more clothing on than he, it was probable that he could pass unnoticed on the city streets.

"Don't worry about it," said Murf, at his question. "This is a shipping town, and they're used to seeing all kinds of people. Even Vikes like you."

"Vikes?"

"You don't even know that, do you? You're a Vike. I can tell by the tin hat. But it's all right. The Brish and the Vikes are at peace right now. Just the same we had better get you some different clothes, because they'll be looking for a Vike when they find we escaped."

"But they didn't know that when I was captured. They asked me if I was Mic or Mac."

"The night-watch is stupid," Murf explained. "But when they tell the prison captain what you looked like, he'll know. So we'd better get rid of that hat."

Regretfully Mark tossed the winged helmet back into the alley, and they proceeded at a leisurely pace down the street— away from the prison.

"Where shall we go?" inquired Mark.

"Leave everything to me," advised Murf. "I've got friends in this city. They'll take care of us." Murf spoke in a tone that any twentieth century ward-heeler would have recognized at once.

Mark decided he might as well go along. He would meet new people, and that would help him remember. Even now his mind was coping with a vagrant memory. It had to do with Murf's assertion that he was a Vike. Earlier in the day, he had told the night-watch that he was a Yank, and though he didn't know why he had said it, it had seemed to be right at the time. But now the word Vike seemed to strike a responsive chord. It wasn't quite right, his memory insisted that the word was "Viking," and it had an air of familiarity.

Suddenly bedlam swooped down upon them.

Around a corner swung an ornate carriage drawn by sleek horses, and flanked on either side by a mounted soldier. Without warning, the horses suddenly reared, kicked at the traces, and dashed madly down the street!

THE MOUNTED soldiers, taken by surprise, were slow to act, and the carriage had a good start before they thundered in pursuit. Their mounts were swift and they were gradually overtaking the runaways, when an excited shout arose from the people lining the street. Directly ahead of the careening carriage was the ox-cart, effectively blocking the way. The soldiers could never close up the gap in time to prevent the crash.

Mark caught a fleeting vision, through the window of the carriage, of a terror-stricken girl with an infant clasped to her breast. Abruptly he went into action.

The nearer horse was opposite him when he made a prodigious leap and landed astride its back. The frightened horse almost went to its knees. Mark made a frantic snatch for the reins of the farther horse as it slewed about, threatening to dash them all against a building. His lightning grasp was sure and in another instant he had brought the heads of both horses back. They came to a stop with several feet of safety short of the impending crash.

Before Mark could realize that he was really quite a remarkable fellow, an excited crowd had rushed him and raised him aloft, shouting and parading around the carriage.

Bewildered, Mark began to notice things. This joyous throng seemed to think that he had done an heroic thing. That might mean that the woman in the carriage was a person of great eminence, and beloved to those who were honoring him.

He noticed on the second time around the carriage that the door was opening and a man, resplendent in a handsome uniform, was getting out. The crowd abruptly stopped and placed him on his feet before the uniformed man, then respectfully stepped back.

The man held out his hand. Erect, still pale from his experience, he gave an impression of intelligence and culture above that of the others around him. There was a kindliness about his eyes that was at once engaging and yet seemed to hide a certain ever-present sadness.

"Your name, my friend?" he asked.

"Mark." He hesitated. "Should I know yours?"

Surprise appeared on the man's face before he could control it. "Perhaps you should," he replied, smiling. "I am Jon, Duke of Scarbor. And I wish to extend my sincere thanks, on behalf of Her Highness and myself, for your heroic act."

Mark nodded, embarrassed and not certain if the customs of this land required him to speak or act in any specified manner toward a man who was obviously one of the ruling class. He liked this man, Jon, and didn't wish to offend him.

"As a token of gratitude, it is my desire to reward you in a way that would be most pleasing to you. Suppose you name the reward. Anything within my power."

There was only one thing he desired, Mark was ruefully thinking, and no man could grant that—the return of his memory.

"There is nothing," he said. "Anyone with the opportunity would have acted as—"

Murf, suddenly pushing his way through the crowd, interrupted him. "Your Highness," he panted, dodging the hands of those who would have stopped him, "there *is* a reward that would please this man!"

CHAPTER IV

KING TO BE

THE DUKE WAVED aside the soldiers who pounced on the red-head before he came within six feet of the carriage. "Speak," he commanded. "What is this reward?"

Murf leered at the soldiers. "A pardon!" he answered, and grinned at the wondering glances of the crowd. "This man comes from a far country. Without knowing of the curfew laws he entered the city too early in the morning. The night-watch clapped him in prison about an hour before the gong. And Your Highness knows the penalty for curfew-breaking."

The Duke shuddered. "Quite. But if he was placed in prison how is it that he is now free?"

"Upon being informed of the penalty he must suffer for his innocent trespass, he escaped. But he will be tracked down without Your Highness' pardon."

The Duke smiled. "I am in your debt for this information," he said. "You have shown me how I may avert a wrong. But how is it that you know all this?"

Murf glanced nervously about as if wondering whether to make a run for it, then squared his thin shoulders. "I also was unjustly imprisoned," he said, trying to look as virtuous as possible. "When I told this man how I was borne false witness, against, he took pity and freed me also."

The Duke's eyes twinkled. "A Mic, eh?" he chuckled. "Always unjustly accused, always downtrodden; but never without a likely sounding story. However, I am in your debt. There will be two pardons and quickly."

A cheer went up from the crowd as the Duke reentered the carriage. But the smile of approval from his pretty wife probably weighed far heavier in his scale of values. Neither could guess that as a ruler, he was inviting disaster.

Mark and Murf were both lifted to the shoulders of enthusiastic men and carried behind the carriage back to the prison. This time they entered the office of the captain, which was much better than being forced through the courtyard to the cellblock.

A short time later Mark hurried toward the alley from which they had earlier emerged to the street. Murf scurried after, quite puzzled. He wasn't kept in suspense long. With a dive Mark swooped into the alley and came out a moment later, smiling happily. He brushed same mud from the gleaming surface of the helmet he had retrieved, and placed it jauntily on his head. Then he patted the axe which had been returned to him. Murf shook his head, mystified.

"It looks like losing them gimcracks is the only thing about the whole business that really had you worried," he remarked.

MARK NODDED. He didn't explain that the axe and the helmet were the only concrete links between him and the past. Nor that it was his hope that the sight and feel of them would stir his memory. And it is just as well that he didn't, for then Murf might have seen that he lost them again. For canny Murf was cooking up a plan, whose ultimate success depended on Mark's innocence and gullibility.

"Why did you lie?" Mark inquired. "You didn't tell me you were falsely accused. And I'll bet you weren't."

Murf laughed. "No. Sure, it just sounded better that way. His nibs didn't believe me anyway. But I couldn't tell him that I was guilty of treason. He wouldn't have pardoned me for that."

Mark thought for a minute. "Then you took a chance of being sent back to prison when you spoke up for me."

Murf waved a hand airily. "Sure. Sure. It was a gamble, but it turned out all right. And I paid back a debt. You got me out, and I got you a pardon."

"Still, you took a dangerous chance. Treason is a grave offense.

Now I'm in your debt." Through Mark's gratitude ran a tiny dark thread of suspicion. Beware the Irish bearing gifts.

Murf glanced away to hide triumph in his face.

"Forget it," he said. "Come on with me."

Mark saw no reason why he shouldn't.

The way led through a squalid section of the town, and little attention was paid to Mark's singular dress—or lack of it. There were sailors from far lands, fish-peddlers with their carts, laborers, an occasional lady of the street, and innumerable strutting soldiers.

Once an armorer in the doorway of his shop stopped Mark and asked for a look at his axe. Mark handed it to him and wondered at the man's excitement.

"The ancient metal!" gasped the armorer. "Where did you get it?"

Mark shook his head, uncertainly. "I've always had it," he answered.

"But it's made of the ancient metal, which does not rust! It is found nowhere but in the ruins of the cities of our ancestors. Modern steel-men cannot duplicate it. How much will you sell it for?"

Mark hesitated, and Murf decided to take a hand. "What will you pay?"

"A thousand coppers!"

Murf turned to Mark. "It's a good price," he said. "You can get an ordinary axe for ten. You'll need money. You haven't any, have you?" He looked hopefully toward Mark's single pocketless garment.

Money… medium of exchange… with which one could buy the necessities of life. No! he decided, abruptly. "I need the axe, but I don't need money. Sorry, no sale."

Murf shook his head and they went on their way. Mark was becoming acutely aware of the fact that somehow or other he required no "necessities of life."

THEIR DESTINATION was a haberdashery shop. The proprietor, a wizened man with shrewd eyes, was both surprised and upset at sight of Murf. He came round the counter, closed the door and pulled curtains across the windows.

"Murf!" he exclaimed, in tones he might have used upon being told that an epidemic had struck the town. "You mustn't come here! They're sure to find you. It will jeopardize the cause!"

Murf laughed. "Hush your blather, man. Is your leader as stupid as you? I have been pardoned. This is Mark, who will some day be our king!" This last announcement came as a distinct surprise to Mark, who had some remembering notion of the word's meaning.

Murf went on rapidly, while Mark listened with incredulous ears. Murf's story proved him to be an accomplished liar and an adept at the perhaps forgotten art of the buildup. The haber-dasher, who was named Smid, listened with avid interest, now and then glancing admiringly at Mark.

"He is a fit leader," Murf concluded, pompously. "One who will administer justice, not persecution."

Smid nodded. "And one who will inspire the cooperation we need from our loosely-joined allies. The other groups have never fully trusted you, you know." His eyes twinkled maliciously.

Murf nodded. "My cursed red hair," he said. "They've always thought I was with the Mics, just because my grandfather came from Eire. The dolts! But they'll trust this Vike, for the Vikes are not intriguers. If they wanted anything from the Brish they'd descend in their ships and take it."

Smid nodded and seemed perfectly willing to accept Mark at face value. Mark, who found his attitude unbelievably naive, followed Murf into the living quarters in the rear.

"Look," he said. "Would you mind explaining all this? I don't know what this is all about, and I'm pretty sure I don't want any part of it. It seems to me you might have the decency to consult me about it before you go around slamming crowns on my head."

Murf looked at him incredulously, and then changed his

expression to a sympathetic smile. "I had forgotten," he said. "You don't know that I'm giving you a chance to help the down-trodden and oppressed. Man, you have not the right to refuse at all. 'Tis your sacred duty. Listen to me."

AND MURF explained. From his deft and Celtic tongue rolled an eloquent depiction of the terrible conditions of the land. Of the unbearable taxation of the poor, and lavish ease and luxury of the nobles. Of the inhuman penal code, torture, corruption, squalor—all dripped persuasively from his flow of words until at last the bewildered Mark was more than half convinced, and sure only of not being sure of anything.

Even apart from his obligation to Murf, Mark really felt that this might be a cause to warrant the aid of any red-blooded man. This thought brought him up short. *His* blood was blue.

Not that it changed his ideas, but it reminded him that he must not lose sight of the fact that he was different, and that he had to find out the reason for the difference. He knew that there lay the clues that would lead him to the lovely lady of his half-awakened memories.

"But you said I would some day be king," he said.

"Of course. The various groups who are working for the betterment of this country, are loosely joined because they lack a real leader. You will supply them with one. They will unite under your leadership."

How was Mark to know that Murf was a master of the patter of the soapbox agitator? He sounded sincere enough and clever words are delicate but often irresistible webs to trap and hold fast the innocent.

"But it doesn't make sense," Mark insisted, yielding inch by inch. "I am an outsider, not even familiar with the country."

"Makes no difference," said Murf. "The Brish are a people who require an impressive leader, or they won't move. They must have a king, even though that king has to relegate all the duties of his kingship to more capable men. The Brish need him as a symbol. And your part in the coming events will be to bind our members under your leadership, and let them revere you as their deliverer. And in the meantime, I, as your lieutenant, will plan the moves to be made."

Mark said nothing.

Murf, who had stripped and was busily washing off some of the prison grime, sensed something of Mark's thoughts. "Your position is an honorable one," he pointed out. "It will further a cause which might otherwise lack the impetus to get it started. If I am willing to continue the work without hope of reward, even of recognition, you should be. To you will go all the glory and adulation. But to remove the yoke of oppression from my people, I consider it a small sacrifice. Surely you can have no objection." His tone was convincingly pious.

Mark suddenly felt ashamed of himself. "I'll work with you," he said simply. "But there is one thing I must insist upon."

"What is that?"

"When this work is done, you must take over yourself. I can't be tied down here. I must be free to take up my life from the point where I lost it. Some day I'll remember, and then I shall leave."

CHAPTER V

MARK THE DELIVERER

THE DAYS THAT followed were busy ones for Mark. Murf and Smid contacted members of rebellious groups in the Duchy of Scarbor, presented Mark, and proceeded to win them over to the idea of a new leader. The idea took hold with unanimous enthusiasm. Stories of Mark's unjust imprisonment, his miraculous escape and the adroit manner in which he had grasped the opportunity to obtain his, and Murf's, pardon, had traveled ahead of them.

The story had lost nothing in the telling, having already been considerably embellished by Murf. He had credited Mark with having planned the whole episode, and with admirable modesty had toned down his own part in it.

Mark allowed this, though inwardly cringing at the deception, for he realized that he was playing a necessary part. Occasionally there would be doubters, who found it impossible to believe that a man's arms could be strong enough to bend stout iron bars. So Mark would patiently show off for them, feeling a little silly. On request, he gave exhibitions of axe throwing, in much the same fashion as twentieth century politicians had gone about kissing babies and submitting to initiation into Indian tribes.

In the course of his campaign Mark ran across many evidences of poverty and oppression, and his anger mounted along with his growing urge to do something about it. Murf and Smid were delighted at the success of his efforts to bring all the rebellious factions under his leadership. His speeches, prepared by Murf, were delivered with fervor, and conviction. Mark was no orator and got fussed when a crowd cheered Murf's canny platitudes, but it was all in the day's work.

The Duchy of Scarbor, of the four that comprised the country of the Brish, was the most important nut to crack. It was the largest and most thickly populated, and it harbored some of the more powerful of the ruling nobles. The Duke of Scarbor, he learned with a twinge of sympathy, was a mere figurehead, forced to do the bidding of the other nobles. They controlled the army and owned the greater part of the land. And although Jon, the duke, made efforts to alleviate suffering among the poorer classes, he was invariably overruled. The nobles, interested only in their own welfare, considered it good policy to keep the people properly to heel.

Lunn, the province to the south, was the capital of the country of the Brish. It was presided over by Aired, Emperor of the Brish, who was the father of Jon of Scarbor. He too, was popular with the people, but helpless to do anything for them. His hands were as thoroughly tied by the Council of Peers, as were his son's by the ruling nobles of Scarbor. This Council, it appeared, were representatives of the various nobles of the four Duchies, empowered to act in their behalf.

But though his success in organization was such that the rebellious factions of the Duchy of Scarbor were solidly united in a matter of days, Mark was troubled by a sense of futility. Time's passage had not produced the desired effect on his memory. The associations which should have reminded him of incidents in his past were failing of their purpose. Could it be that he was living a life so foreign to his former one that there were no parallels, no similar occurrences that he might match up and start a train of recollection?

THERE WAS only one thing to console him in his constant quest for knowledge of his past. During the long nights when his companions rested and slept, he was able to think more clearly. Each night he was in a different place, as they campaigned about the country, but his surroundings meant little to him. For no matter where he was, he could always conjure up the vision of Nona, the woman he knew was his.

And lately he was able to associate her with the presence of another person. Who this person was he couldn't quite grasp, but the feeling was there that it was someone who had played an important part in his former life. And Nona was clearer, too. Sometimes he could hear the low throbbing of her laugh, and it never failed to leave him with a sensation of happiness and desire.

The Duchy of Scarbor had been thoroughly canvassed and thoroughly organized by the end of the second week of the harvest holidays. The final week of the holiday period was to be devoted to games in the great arena. These games were a gesture of the nobles calculated to take the minds of their subjects off their troubles.

Murf and Smid decided that inasmuch as the following days would bring a return to normalcy, it was high time to strike their blow.

First all prisoners must be released from the jails. Most of these would immediately join the cause and swell their ranks. It was decided that the first jail delivery would be made from the prison from which he and Mark had escaped.

Murf laid his plans with admirable thoroughness. Instead of going about the business furtively, he dressed several men in uniforms corresponding to, those of the night-watch. Mark was attired in a sergeant's outfit, except that he insisted on keeping his axe.

Boldly they marched through the streets long after curfew, headed for the jail. The night was cloudy and the moon obscured. This fitted their plans, for after the jailbreak it would be necessary for the prisoners to scatter and find concealment with friends, and every minute on the streets there would be danger of being sighted by genuine patrolmen.

The plan went off like clockwork—up to a certain point.

Reaching the prison the party entered the courtyard and stopped before the huge oaken door. Mark hammered on it with the butt of his axe. The door was supposedly impregnable to anything less devastating than a battering ram, and could only be opened from inside the guardroom. The inner door was equally formidable from the side of the cell block. It also could be opened from the guardroom only.

But evidently the authorities had never considered that a weakness was present in the fact that the guards were in the habit of opening the outer door whenever the night-watch brought in a prisoner. The open-sesame was the hammering of the night-watch sergeant's club.

After a moment the door swung outward. Before the startled guard knew what was happening, he was felled by an enthusiastic club. His three companions were downed before they could move.

A ring of keys hung on a nail beside the inner door. In a matter of moments Mark had swung open the inner door and released the prisoners. A search of the prison revealed several other blocks of cells, one to match each key on the ring. The locks on the doors of each row of cells were opened by a single key. Over two hundred prisoners were released in the course of less than a half hour.

THE THING had been accomplished with the utmost quiet. Mark was congratulating himself on their efficiency when he received a rude jolt. In the guardroom were only three unconscious men!

Hastily he gave orders to leave. He didn't know how much time had elapsed since the missing man had regained consciousness. He may have already summoned help. Why hadn't he taken time to bind them or at least have left a guard over them?

But there was no time now for regrets. He swung the outer door open, and realized at once that the damage had been done. The sound of a large number of running men echoed down the street!

They were nearing the archway that led into the courtyard. In the few seconds that remained, Mark put into effect the only plan that had a chance of success. He deployed his men in the shadows at the sides of the archways. The door to the guardroom gaped open, illuminated by a glow from the oil-lamp within.

It was Mark's hope that the approaching men would head immediately for the door, and that they would fail to see his men in the darkness outside.

The sound of slapping sandals was growing louder, and Mark's heart sank as he heard the occasional clank of armor. Sword-hilts striking against breastplates! These were soldiers coming, not poorly armed watchmen. His eyes, accustomed to the darkness, could see the grim expressions on the faces of his men, indicating that they had interpreted the sounds as he had.

But the way they held their clubs and knives told him, that even though outnumbered and outclassed in armament, they would give a good accounting of themselves if it came to a fight.

The foremost of the soldiers dashed through the archway and continued, without breaking his stride, toward the lighted door. His eyes, partially blinded by the dim light, missed the men crouched in the shadows. Those who followed dashed right after him.

A steady stream, numbering at least fifty armored soldiers, crossed the courtyard at a run. Mark was elated at the success of his strategy. He was calling for his men to break cover and make their escape when abruptly a laggard soldier puffed through the archway. He was a heavy man, and had little breath left when he confronted Mark's party. But what small amount of wind he retained, he used in a hoarse yell as he drew his sword and swung it at Mark.

Mark stepped out of range of the swing and then felled the man with an axe blow as his momentum carried him past. But the yell had done its work. The last two of the soldiers to dash into the prison had heard it and were calling to those who had gone before.

One man went down without striking a blow, but the other three were cutting at him viciously. His own men were not slow in sizing up the situation, however. In a body they dashed forward and belabored the three with heavy clubs. The soldiers were driven back through the portal. It slammed shut with a thud.

MARK REALIZED that he was holding a lion by the tail. He leaned against the door and kept it closed against the pressure of the soldiers on the other side. But there was no way to secure it. The bolts were on the other side of the door, In a few minutes, as the men on the inside found that the prison was empty, they would all be pushing.

"Back to headquarters!" he ordered. "Walk! Don't attract any attention. I'll hold the door until you get a good start."

"But what of you? They'll get you!"

"Do as I say! If we all make a break for it, they'll trace us back to headquarters. Go quietly and no one will notice you. I'll meet you there."

Reluctantly, the spurious night-watch obeyed. His way was the only solution.

Mark, his back braced against the door, counted the beats of his pulse.

He had to give his party a start sufficient to carry them far enough away that they could not be reached if the soldiers should spread out in a search for them.

At the count of five hundred, indicating that about seven minutes had passed, he suddenly released his pressure from the door, and sped across the courtyard.

The door swung violently open and five men went to their knees. Those in the rear scrambled past them and took up the chase.

But by the time they reached the archway, Mark was a dwindling figure in the distance. At their best speed the soldiers followed. It was a hopeless chase, for in the space of a few blocks the murkiness of the night had swallowed up their quarry, leaving no evidence of his passing.

They scattered, trying to pick up the trail, but finally had to give it up. The search ended at a spot several miles removed from the location of the rebel headquarters, for Mark had purposely led them in the opposite direction. But the real chase was only beginning....

CHAPTER VI

LORN LADY

A VIKING SHIP of the eightieth century, while a model of efficiency for its day, was no speedboat. And so it was that after two weeks of sailing, Nona's ship was still plowing earnestly but sluggishly through the North Se. It had been a long voyage, especially without the companionship of Mark. Even at his noblest and most irritating, Mark was more fun than any other man. And she missed him. She fretted too; knowing Omega's capacity for getting Mark into trouble, she almost wished he wouldn't find Mark. Omega, you see, was the typical friend of the family, only instead of luring Mark off on disgraceful benders, he was more apt to drag him into perilous crusades to save the world.

Most of Nona's life had been spent so far from the sea that her only knowledge of it had come from books. And the few months that she had traveled on the water had been in Mark's company. Without him, she found she didn't like the sea so very much. It was too unruly, too desolate—and too darned big.

Her mind kept returning to the morning when she had found that he had been washed overboard. She experienced over and over again the wild grief of that moment, and the hopelessness of the subsequent search.

Long days had passed without hearing further from Omega and the strength of her hope was wearing thin. So omnipotent were the powers of Omega that if her husband still lived, the Selenite should have found him long ago. Daily the conviction was becoming stronger in her mind that the visit of Omega had been a figment of her overwrought imagination.

On the fifteenth day land was sighted.

Among the Norsemen there came a stir of excitement. Sven, the captain, climbed the mast and took his place beside the lookout. It was up to him to determine their position. For although they had set their course to bring them to their home port at Stadtland, there was no guarantee that the land sighted was within a hundred miles of that point. Norsemen navigated by instinct—they were very proud of their intuitive sea bearings. But in point of fact, instinct seemed to be merely another name for trial and error.

Sven, who did know every jutting cape and twisting inlet along the coast of his own land, even if he was pretty blank on other coasts, quickly discovered that the ship had made an extraordinarily lucky landfall and lay within one day's northward travel of its destination.

Nona watched listlessly as the crew bent enthusiastic backs to the long oars, aiding the feeble wind that refused to belly the great sail. The sight of land had brought no stir to her breast, in spite of the weary weeks that had made her utterly fed up with the sea.

For although an honored place in Norse society would be hers, by reason of Mark's attainments, the prospect seemed savorless without him to share it.

Of late she had spent most of her time shut in her cabin. The cheerful faces of the crew irked her. They felt none of the doubts that were making her miserable. She had told them, as Omega had suggested, that she had been the recipient of a message from Thor the Thunder God, who had told her that Mark was engaged in fulfilling a mission that would take him several weeks, but that he would return to them when it was accomplished. The Vikings, who revered Mark as the chosen of Thor, found the deception quite believable, and felt no more anxiety for Mark's safety.

This gullibility gave Nona a low opinion of their intelligence, and she found it impossible to endure their light-hearted conversation. She was not by any means certain that she would ever again see the face of her husband.

Another thing that made her visits on deck become shorter as the days went by, was the fact that they made her miss Mark all the more. Invariably he had been with her when she left the cabin. As a pastime he had taught her the use of the axe and short-sword. Garbed in the heavy leather trapping of the Norsemen, to protect them from cuts that might spill too much of their radio-active blood, they would spend hours cutting and slashing at each other, in mock combat.

AT FIRST they had been very careful not to hurt each other, and had used axes and swords with dulled cutting edges. Mark, during this phase of her tuition, had concentrated on the finer

*Mark's eyes glared defiance, even while
the smoke curled up from his chest*

points of the art, teaching her to fend off axe slashes with deft
parries of the shortsword held in the left hand, and to deliver
effective counter-slashes.

And for some time he had dealt his blows lightly, afraid of
hurting her. But as her skill increased and it became apparent
that she was as proof against injury as he, her strength and agil-
ity made him extend himself more and more.

The time soon came when they battled with such skill and
fervor that the crew looked on aghast at the apparent intensity
of the conflict.

Both of them tireless, they could maintain their strenuous
exercise at fever pitch, long after the hardiest of the Norsemen
would have fallen, exhausted. The battles invariably ended in one
way. Mark would lead her to swing for his helmet while his guard
was down, then in the instant she was off balance, he would drop
his weapons, make a lightning lunge and swing her high in the
air, unable to touch him with either axe or sword. Laughing
and bowing, they would acknowledge the wild applause of the
conflict-loving Vikings.

But now that Mark was gone, the very things which had

brought so much happiness made her heart ache. Her misery had to remain locked within her, for there was no one in whom she could confide. The cabin was her only refuge from the care-free cheerfulness of these simple men. And it was to the cabin that she turned after Sven came down from the rigging with news of their location.

She opened the door, froze for an instant into rigid immobility, then abruptly stepped inside and closed the door after her.

There, reclining on a cushioned divan, in a pose that would have done credit to a member of the seraglio from which the divan had been pilfered, was Omega. He was presenting himself in the same antiquated body that she had last seen. With his bony chin cupped seductively in the interlaced fingers of scrawny hands, he treated her to a toothless grin—a grin which might have been bold and dashing if the body he had acquired had been about fifty years younger. As it was, he just looked silly.

"Hullo, babe," he said.

"Where's Mark?"

"Let's not go into that right now," he urged. "I was just thinking maybe I could take his place for a while. You're not a bad-looking wench, you know." He ogled her shamelessly.

Nona looked sour. "You're not very, funny," she stated. "Where *is* Mark?"

Omega allowed a tear to trickle from the corner of his left eye. The right one still retained a twinkle. It was a special delight of his to create human bodies and then make them do hideously inhuman things.

"Whatever that is you're doing with your eyes, stop it. It's disgusting. And so, you Selenite lecher, are you. Where's Mark?"

"So you still want him?" His voice quavered with emotion. "When you could have a fine specimen of vigorous manhood like me, for the asking. A sad case…. Yes, a very sad case." At this point Nona showed signs of becoming violent. Omega sobered abruptly. "All right, all right. I found him."

"Take me to him," she demanded.

"Not so fast," he counseled, waving her to a seat. "I found him, all right, over a week ago. And a tough job it was. But I don't think it would be a good idea to take you to him just now."

Nona's face fell, "Doesn't he want… Has he forgotten me?"

OMEGA STROKED his chin. "That's the funny thing about it. He struck his head when he went overboard. He remembers you, but he's forgotten everything else. When I finally found him, I took the liberty of delving into his mind, a thing I seldom do—don't consider it ethical. But I had to learn what had happened.

"And it turns out that he remembers your name, and can visualize you in his mind, but he doesn't even know who you are! He has only a dim conviction that you belong to him, but that's all."

"But can't you restore his memory? Or bring him here? He'll remember if you do that."

"Wouldn't be advisable," Omega said. "His brain is healing and it would be better to let his memory return by itself. Besides, he's started a job that he must finish…."

"Now, Omega, you listen to me," she began. "If you encourage Mark into any more crazy adventures, I'll—I'll scratch your eyes out! Or whomsoevers eyes those unmatched horrors are." Omega paid no attention.

He went on to explain how Mark had swum, after falling overboard, to the shore of the land that had once been ancient England; how he had become embroiled in the cause of the rebels, and that after seeing the privations suffered by the lower classes—the undernourished children, the fear of parents for their daughters—he wouldn't stop his campaign for anything, even the return of his memory.

"Then you can take me to him," said Nona. "I can help him. I think it's crazy—but if I can't stop him, I'm going to be with him."

"No!" Omega emphasized the word by jumping up and down in fury.

"Why not?" asked Nona, using her most beguilingly reasonable tone.

"It wouldn't be safe."

"Nonsense! I'm the equal of any five men. Mark taught me to fight, you know."

Omega grinned ruefully. "Yes, I know. Mark trained you. I don't get any credit for providing the blood that made it possible, do I? But I wasn't thinking of *your* safety. I wouldn't worry about you in a cave full of snarling tigers. It's Mark. Right now Mark is doing very well, and he's slowly getting an inkling of his past. But if you were suddenly to pop up, he would be torn between a desire to look after you, and the necessity of finishing what he has started. And he'd probably wind up in the hands of the enemy, who aren't at all nice to rebels."

The battle was joined. Nona insisted she would be more help than hindrance, while Omega was determined that she finish the journey to Stadtland and prepare a home for Mark on his eventual return to the land of the Norsemen.

Finally Omega, wearying of the yammer, abruptly deserted the form of the aged man and became the spiderlike creature which represented his original body. He then made a noise which could have been made only with human lips, and followed it with the remark: "Phooey to females!" This was taking a nasty advantage but ethics had never been Omega's strong point. Nona shrieked in terror, sank back on a divan, and Omega disappeared entirely. "Come back here, you—you thing," she raged. "That's not fair!" She began to heave cushions about the room.

She tired of this in a few minutes, and sat up to stare at the wall of the cabin. Then, after a few deft touches to her wavy ebon hair, she stepped out on the deck.

Shortly after, she and Sven were poring over his inaccurate maps of the islands of the North Sea. Nona had invented a plan. It appeared that Thor had sent her a second message.

CHAPTER VII

THE FAT SATAN

MARK STRODE ALONG a cobbled street a full mile to the west of the misleading route he had taken when the soldiers were pursuing him. He was doubling back now, heading in the general direction of Smid's haberdashery shop. He was walking slowly and smiling happily to himself. The smile was not occasioned by the success of the jail delivery. Nor was it a result of his coup in drawing the pursuit away from the rebel headquarters. Both things had left his mind entirely.

He was remembering!

From the instant his party of disguised rebels had entered the prison courtyard he had felt a vague stirring in his brain. It had congealed into concrete thought when he had hammered on the door.

Two weeks before he had experienced a return of certain portions of his memory when he had stood on that very spot. The association had brought it back. On the other occasion his thoughts had been driven away by his sudden surge of anger at the foul blow of one of the night watchmen. But this time, even though events had been happening with bewildering rapidity, the train of his thoughts had continued, falteringly but unbroken.

First as he had hammered at the huge portal, had come the memory of days of intense abdominal pain.

Coupled with the recollection he could see a face, a somber face which he knew belonged to Dr. Kelso. Old Chisel-chin, he had called him. The doctor was going to remove the pain. It had been vague and disquieting, at first, this memory.

But it had strengthened suddenly as the party waited at the door.

In a matter of seconds he had experienced the return of memories covering thousands of years. Dr. Kelso had developed a new anaesthetic which had apparently worked admirably on guinea-pigs. He had wished Mark's signed permission to use it during the appendectomy which must be performed. The permission had been granted, with surprising results. Mark had slipped quietly into a state of suspended animation from which he had been awakened six thousand years later by the former inhabitant of the moon, Omega.

Good old Omega. Mark's grin broadened. He wondered where that moon-imp was now. Probably considered his work on Earth finished, now that he had safely established Mark and Nona as the new Adam and Eve of a new and finer race, and gone cavorting about the other planets. Mark frowned. Everything had gone wrong; Omega wouldn't like it. Mark and Nona were separated and here he was all mixed up in some insular revolution that might very well be considerably less altruistic than its ringleaders made it out. Wherever Omega was, Mark fervently hoped that Omega wasn't paying any too much attention to what he, Mark, was up to.

Then suddenly Mark knew that the thing he wanted most in life was Nona. Remembering the howling storm which had washed him overboard he felt sudden anxiety for her safety. But it was allayed immediately by the thought that the stout Viking ship would have weathered the dying fury of that tempest with ease. And Nona had been safe in their cabin. Still, the thought of her safety was not enough.

ABRUPTLY HE was cursing himself for becoming so engrossed in his thoughts as to lose awareness of his surroundings. In his preoccupation he had been totally oblivious to the fact that his movements had been observed and that he was being slowly but completely surrounded by a body of soldiers.

In the darkness of the night they managed to get quite close before he noticed them. It is likely that one of them would have stolen close enough to strike an unexpected blow, if Mark hadn't been warned by the clanking rattle of a breastplate. As it was, when he did sense their presence they were on all sides.

Viciously he snatched his axe from its holster and leaped for the nearest warrior. The surprised soldier went down without even making an attempt to defend himself.

The next few minutes tore the silence of the night into shattered fragments. With a whirling attack that dazzled the soldiers with its speed and ferocity Mark plied his axe in a dozen directions at once. So baffling was his footwork and so vicious his handling of the axe that it was some minutes before they were able to so much as touch him with a weapon.

The first cut he received, a shallow one on the shoulder, was a poor retaliation for the seven men he had laid on the ground.

But there was one among the soldiers who evidently had more intelligence than the others. That man was their sergeant. In the hectic moments that Mark was striking down one after another of his men, he realized that unless a lucky blow brought him down, this amazing fellow might very well wipe out his whole command. The sergeant had been carefully drilled, but clearly this was no time to be too picky about regulations. Standing well back out of Mark's darting lunges, he waited for his opportunity. It came when he saw Mark deliver a smashing blow to the man directly in front of him and then whirl to face those at his back.

In that instant the sergeant dove, catching both of Mark's legs in his crushing embrace. Mark toppled to the ground.

WITHOUT HESITATION they all jumped at the chance to climb aboard. Mark felt as if the Notre Dame eleven with a full complement of substitutes were jumping up and down on his midriff. For a few minutes Mark heaved beneath the weight of their bodies, but he became more docile when the point of a knife pricked his throat and a stern voice commanded him to be still.

The soldiers brought stout ropes and bound him. Several grumbled because they wanted to slice his throat right then and the sergeant wouldn't let them. To the survivors fell the task of carrying Mark as well as their fallen comrades.

Mark was seething as he was carried roughly through the city streets. Like a bale of dirty laundry. Occasionally the men holding his feet would lower him enough that he bounced for several steps on the cobbles. This seemed to give them considerable satisfaction, though they stopped it when they noticed that Mark didn't seem to be paying any attention. Even though he was in the throes of an intense rage, Mark wasn't oblivious to his surroundings. He wouldn't make that mistake again. And he noticed, wonderingly, that his captors weren't carrying him in the direction of the jail.

He noticed further that none of the soldiers were familiar. They certainly weren't of the same group that he had encountered earlier that night. For although the light had been poor, he surely would have recognized at least one of them. These men were all strangers.

"Where are you taking me?" he asked the sergeant.

"You'll find out soon enough," came the growled answer. Another one laughed in a sinister sort of way and Mark didn't feel like asking any more questions for a while.

"Where did you fellows learn to tackle like that?" he inquired a little later.

The sergeant expanded. "Never learned it anywhere," he said. "It seemed to be the only way to bring you down. When they want to promote a man to be a sergeant, they always pick the one who can figure a way to meet any circumstance." He cast a disdainful glance at the men around him. "That's why these nitwits aren't sergeants. They're only butchers, and bad ones at that."

Mark nodded. "Your master knows men," he observed. "Who is he?"

"Erlayok," said the sergeant, proudly. "The greatest of them all. He's the real boss around here."

Mark mentally translated this into "Earl of York", and tried to remember what he had heard of the man. Murf had informed him of the status of the various nobles with whom they would have to contend, and as he remembered, the Earl of York was the most powerful of them all. His army was the best equipped, and his lands were the richest.

And he was the most feared, for he maintained a corps of spies who kept him informed of the actions of his enemies, who were legion.

Once again since setting foot on this land of the Brish, Mark found himself spending the night in a dungeon. This time, however, he wasn't incarcerated in an ordinary prison. His cell was one of a dozen in the lower basement of a pretentious palace. Though situated in the confines of the city of Scarbor, it was guarded and fortified with all the elaborate contrivances of a medieval castle. There was no moat, but its lack was well compensated by a high stone wall, its top patrolled by guards.

Nor was Mark left alone to utilize his strength in an effort to break out. A guard with a long, sharp-pointed pike was stationed outside his cell. At Mark's attempt to communicate with him, he obligingly opened his mouth and displayed the place where his tongue had been torn out. Mark shuddered and held his peace.

But Mark had never been much of a hand at just sitting still. He decided to try an experiment. He grasped the bars of the door and began to exert pressure. The guard grinned at the attempt and spat contemptuously. Then he blinked and passed a hand over his eyes. The bars were slowly bending, warping the door.

Instantly the guard sprang into action. Holding his spike like a billiard cue, he jabbed at Mark's hand. The point sunk deep in the flesh of its heel, but his amazing prisoner waved his hand in the air and resumed his prodigious labor. Frantically the guard jabbed at the knuckles. Mark, afraid that the heavy pike would break a bone, stepped back.

The bars were warped appreciably, but not nearly enough to let him through. The guard, mouthing sharp querulous sounds,

stood ready to repel any further attempt. His eyes were express-
ing the amazement he couldn't voice. They were glued unbe-
lievingly on Mark's hands, which showed no signs of a wound.

THE NIGHT wore on, Mark alert for any relaxing on the part
of the guard. But that astounded individual kept rigidly prepared
to use his pike on a moment's notice. When the throbbing gongs
announced the termination of curfew, the man was ready to drop
from exhaustion.

Mark still watched him, sympathetically.

Shortly after curfew there was a commotion in the corridor, and a squad of soldiers made their way to Mark's cell. They
wore enameled-armor with the crest of the Earl's private guard.
Each carried a drawn sword and seemed willing, even anxious,
to use it.

The face of the guard eloquently spoke his relief at getting
rid of his prisoner.

The soldiers surrounded Mark and marched him away. Two
of them were pointing knives directly at his throat. Word of his
prowess had obviously gotten around.

The way led upward, and several flights of stairs were climbed.
Each of these seemed to be of smoother material, the last flight
being constructed of beautifully polished marble. The upper
floors were evidently the living quarters of the earl and his retinue.

A door was opened, a corridor ornamented with carved woods
and tapestries was traversed, and Mark was thrust into a richly
decorated room. The soldiers stopped and stood at attention.

The room, which was furnished to a king's taste, had one
occupant, Erlayok. The man was of massive physique, layered
with pounds and pounds of fat. Yet he gave an impression of
having tremendous power. One could guess that some years
before he had been a commanding figure. For even with all
his gross bulk there was an air of proud austerity about him,
demanding respect from any and all. Mark found himself studying the man carefully.

"At ease," said the Earl. "You may go."

A soldier in the trappings of a captain stuttered and finally found his voice. "Excellency," he said. "This man is as dangerous as a wild boar. It would be better—"

Erlayok silenced him with a glance, a glance that had a deadly threat in it. "You would advise *me?*" he said, softly and slowly: "When you know that these hands have strangled even the beast of which you speak."

The captain blanched visibly, then bowed and withdrew, his men following. A gargantuan roar of laughter tumbled from the Earl's gaping mouth.

Mark flexed the muscles of his shoulders. The more he saw of Erlayok, the less he liked him. But dislike did not breed contempt. The softness of the layers of fat was not reflected in his face, Mark noticed. The face was one of unusual hardness, an inflexible hardness that seemed to reveal the power that was inherent in the man. And it revealed intelligence as well. In the wide-spread, level eyes there was reflected a self-assured wisdom that gave Mark the impression that the man was learned beyond the average of his times. But if there was intelligence, it was a cruel intelligence, not sympathetic, not tolerant of any form of weakness.

"You are the man of whom my spies speak," began Erlayok, contemptuously. "The man who would be king! Do you not know that we have a king, and that he is but a puppet? And that we are satisfied to have it so?"

MARK SAID nothing. He was meditating, trying to decide if it wouldn't be smart to kill Erlayok while he had the chance. Mark had intended that the eventual rebellion be as bloodless as possible. His plans were already laid whereby the nobles and their families would be made useful citizens, and not slaughtered out of hand, as some of his allies favored.

But this man was undoubtedly their most dangerous foe; and to kill him now would save bloodshed later. His death would tend to cripple the nobles by removing their greatest support.

And certainly this man could never be either an ornament to or a useful member of any well regulated society.

"Speak, man!" cried Erlayok, his voice rising a note.

Mark smiled disarmingly. "You seem very confident of your ability to handle me," he observed. "Overconfidence has filled many a cemetery."

Erlayok laughed again. Mark wondered uneasily if there might not be a touch of madness in him. His laughter had a horrible quality, a sort of bubbling, that made Mark's ordinarily steady nerves jitter.

"How true," agreed Erlayok, the laughter subsiding. He sobered. "And it will probably hold good in your case too."

That about decided Mark. Erlayok was just asking for it. Killing him would not be murder. It would be only the execution of a criminal who deserved it many times over. Only five feet separated him from the hideous grossness that was the Erlayok, and Mark poised on the balls of his feet for the leap.

Then abruptly he realized that Erlayok's eyes were beating him back! His feet were solidly on the floor and he had no will to leap.

Mark had experienced this same thing once before, but on that occasion he had been expecting it and had fought back. Now he was beaten down, his senses reeling, before he knew that he was facing a master hypnotist.

Dimly he heard the soft voice: "And you thought I was a creature of physical force only!" It mocked him, and with its dying sound he felt consciousness go.

CHAPTER VIII

DUEL OF TWO CENTURIES

WHEN HE AWOKE he was sitting on the floor, heavy manacles and chains binding his hands and feet. Nothing else had changed. Erlayok sat motionless in his cushioned chair, his heavy chin resting on a heavy fist, and there was no other person in the room.

Mark glanced curiously at the chains and found them to be thin but strong looking. Erlayok was gazing at him, apparently with keen interest, and perhaps with even a touch of amiability.

"You can break them, I don't doubt," he said. "But before you could accomplish it, I would have you unconscious again. So let's be friendly and talk. Perhaps you would like a bit of this wine?"

He gestured toward a bottle and glasses on a small table at his side. Mark shook his head. Turning on the charm, was he?

"You are a man of intelligence," stated Erlayok. "While I held you in a trance I probed into your mind, plumbing to the earliest of your memories. I was astounded. Truly astounded. I could scarcely believe the things I found. That you have lived for many thousands of years; of this mental creature, Omega; and of your adventures in the north country. Yes, there are many things of which we must talk."

"Why?" growled Mark, concealing his own astonishment that this man of modern Britain should possess such power.

In an age when humanity was slowly accomplishing its weary climb back to the heights it had attained in his early youth, it was almost unbelievable that there could exist a man of such mental attainment.

Yet all through history there had been evidences that here and there existed super-intelligences. Babylon, Egypt, Greece and Rome all had their oracles, their necromancers, their prophets, all men of undoubted genius. Men who had astounded the peoples of their times. And today, the phenomenon could happen again, could it not? There was no sense conjecturing. It *had* happened.

"Why?" repeated Erlayok, uncertainly. "But of course, I had forgotten. You are the leader of the rebels. You disapprove of our form of government. My boy, you are being silly. I see I underrated you. With some common ground upon which to meet, you and I could be of great help to each other."

Mark thought that highly unlikely. "How?" he asked.

"First let us discuss the meeting ground," said Erlayok, amiably. "You must know that I am a great scholar. That I have read of the troublous times in which you lived. Certain books are preserved even to this day, and others have been copied. So that scholars, such as myself, have a fair idea of how people lived. And I think that I can show you that things are not so very different right now."

A short burst of sardonic laughter passed Mark's lips.

"Don't laugh too soon," admonished Erlayok. "Of course there are no carts that roll at lightning speed without oxen or horses. Nor are there ships which sail without sails, or machines that fly in the air. But there are still taxes collected that the government may maintain public works, such as an adequate army. That is the same, and I think that is the very thing to which you object."

"Of course I object," Mark retorted. "The bulk of that wealth is not used for public works, but only so you can keep your power, and live in ease and luxury."

"Not the bulk, my boy; only about the same proportion that was used for the purpose by your own governments. Didn't the ones in power in your day divert some of the public funds to their own ends? Didn't they invariably cause legislation to be passed which would benefit themselves? And was this practice frowned upon to the extent that people would take up arms and risk their lives to stop it?"

MARK WAS stumped for a minute. This wise-eyed noble had placed his finger on a sore spot. "Yes," to that he suddenly answered. "People did rebel at times."

"So they did. But when the rebellion was won, did conditions change? Did the new crowd conduct themselves in an exemplary manner? Or did they change things about a little, and then drift back into the old rut?"

Mark saw his argument thrown back in his face. Erlayok was right. The thing had happened many times. "But in my time people didn't work from dawn to dusk and then half starve to death."

"Perhaps not, but then your fine machines enabled you to produce goods in a shorter space of time. The only way to ease things today for the common herd would be to abolish our armies. And we can't do that or our enemies would conquer us and we would be worse off than before.

"So you see that mankind's most expensive luxury is not the ruling class, which charges enough for its services that it may live in ease and comfort, but rather its own belligerence and greed. Man's own vices keep him slaving to satisfy them."

"I don't see how the expense could be so high that your people should have to work every minute of their waking hours to earn a mere existence."

"But it is. Our armies must be large. There are the Macs on the north and the Mics to the west, besides a long coastline to defend against possible attack from your friends, the Norse. I think that just about takes care of our differences of opinion. You can readily see that any change must obviously be for the worse."

Erlayok's suave amiability, his utter logic, and the neatness with which he compared present-day practices with the injustices of Mark's own time, had Mark losing ground fast. But a few of the things he had seen for himself in the past two weeks came to his rescue.

"I suppose you can condone the rape of peasant girls by members of your army," he suggested. "Or perhaps the barbaric treatment of accused prisoners, and the medieval punishments you mete out for minor offenses. Not to mention your delightful practice of torture to obtain confessions."

ERLAYOK SHRUGGED his massive form deprecatively. "Just standards of the times," he said. "Deplorable, I'll admit, but nothing can be done about it. These people are barbarians. You must have seen that."

"How could they help but be—and nothing can be done as long as you don't wish it," flared Mark. "You coddle your army by letting it ride rough-shod over the rights of the very people who work to feed it. The other tear-'em-and-teach-'em stuff goes because you're afraid that if you ever showed the velvet glove inside the steel fist you'd have a swell rebellion on your hands."

Erlayok's eyes hardened for the merest instant. But so flickerlingly that Mark wasn't sure that any change had taken place.

"Tut tut," Erlayok replied. "You are wrought up over nothing. Our people are hardy, used to long hours of labor and poor food. They don't think anything of serving a few months imprisonment for an anti-social act. If we instituted soft punishment, crime would run wild. Punishment must be severe. We nobles are not inherently cruel. Our harshness is forced upon us."

"I notice that you let your soldiers do pretty much as they please," Mark pointed out.

Erlayok spread the fingers of his pudgy—but curiously powerful—hands, in a gesture meant to convey his helplessness in the matter. "Our enemies are powerful," he said. "And it was a recognized fact even in your civilized times that the more bestial a man was, the better soldier he made.

"There was a great general called the Duke of Wellington who said that he preferred men who were bestial and unruly. He said that they made the best soldiers just because their passions were primitive and unbridled. And because they lacked imagination. Such men don't picture their own blood wetting the battlefield. In their fighting rage they think of nothing but the damage they are going to inflict on the enemy. And so they are the more ferocious. We must have that kind of man if we are to survive, and the women know what to expect.

"But let's not discuss it any more. I have shown you that conditions are not essentially different, whatever the age. People must pay for the services their own folly requires. When they elevate themselves to the point that they no longer wish to war on each other; when they become so civilized that they no longer commit crimes against each other; then they will reap the rewards of their own virtue.

"They will no longer have to do ninety percent of their labor in support of expensive armies and police forces. So let us get the most out of our fortunate meeting, and exchange the knowledge that each of us has acquired. We are too wise not to be friends. Am I not right?"

Mark grinned at the term "fortunate meeting." But his eyes narrowed as he remembered his first estimate of the man who now seemed so amiable and friendly.

"If I should agree," he inquired, "just what do you want me to tell you?" Warning bells jangled a persistent alarm in his brain.

"Oh, there are many things I would like to know of your era. Our knowledge, unfortunately, has been gleaned from histories and stories. Legend. It is too general to be of much use. No technical books have ever been found. We don't even know what caused such a loss of knowledge. There must have been thousands of libraries. We have found none."

"War," Mark supplied. "But just what sort of technical knowledge are you after?"

Erlayok was taken off guard by the matter-of-fact way the question was asked. "The thing we need most is a knowledge of the manufacture of guns. Another valuable thing would be the engines which were used to drive armored tanks. We have men skilled in the manufacture of machines, gears and other equipment of the sort. But we have no power to drive machinery; only man and horse power. I've seen a picture of the armored tank of the ancients, and a few of them would drive our enemies off the face of the earth."

ERLAYOK HAD a faraway expression on his face as he pictured the destruction he could create with these weapons. But he snapped alert when he noticed the gleam in Mark's eyes.

"Don't misunderstand me," he hastened to explain. "I want these things because they would relieve our people of the constant fear of invasion which threatens them. Think, man, if we had such things we could drive the Mics back to their island in the west. We could defeat the Macs in the north.

"They would never dare attack us again, and our people would be freed of the burden of taxes required to maintain our present tremendous armies. A skeleton force would be sufficient to keep our enemies at bay."

Mark laughed a short, bitter laugh. "It would never occur to you to defeat your enemies and then use the weapons for further conquest, of course." The irony was not subtle.

Erlayok tried hard to look like a man who has been grossly insulted. He leaned back in his chair and shook his head sadly.

"Friend," he said, "you malign me. But I can understand. You have been here for only a few days and you have seen only one side of our life. And so you have judged harshly. But see this map."

Lightly, for a man of his tremendous weight, Erlayok strode to one wall and ripped aside a tapestry. Beneath it was a large map of the British Isles. Mark, chains clanking, heaved himself up off the floor and examined it closely. He deduced from the accuracy of its meridians that it was a copy of some ancient map that had been found in the ruins of one of the old cities. But there was nothing ancient about its other markings. It was a modern map in every respect.

Erlayok had said something about driving the Mics back to their island in the west. This had been Mark's first inkling that any of the land formerly known as England had been encroached upon. Now he got a new surprise from the map.

It depicted the area held by the Mics as being larger than that of the Brish. The Mics' eastern border made a curved line through the sites of the ancient cities of Manchester and Birmingham, touching the town of Weymouth at its southern extremity. All this in addition to their native isle. And just as surprising, was the southern border of the Macs. It crossed the island diagonally from Lancaster to Stockton. Truly the land of the Brish had shrunken.

"You will note," Erlayok pointed, "that the boundaries we must protect are long, and hard to defend. The Mics, who are naturally combative and quite numerous, have been pushing forward, a little piece at a time, for hundreds of years. And the Macs as well. It requires constant vigilance and a large army, or they would engulf us."

"You say they are numerous," observed Mark. "Certainly not as numerous as the Brish. I remember England as a thickly populated island. Far more people to the square mile than your enemies. In fact, that is probably the reason why the Brish were originally able to take over the rule of these peoples."

"Today," claimed Erlayok, "we are outnumbered three to one." He paused, and a gleam came in his eyes. "You say the Brish once controlled these people who are now our enemies? Then their lands are rightfully ours!"

"No more than your lands belong to them," said Mark. "If you go back far enough all three peoples were independent, each occupying separate territories." He remembered about the Germans in East Prussia, about Alsace and the Sudeten and the Austro-Italian Tyrol, and knew that that argument was hopeless.

MARK WONDERED why the Brish should be so outnumbered. Then he thought of the wars which had smashed the civilized world he had known. England, with its railway centers and important industries, had probably been the scene of the most devastating battles. Its large cities, housing millions, had been the targets of far more bombings than the less important and less thickly populated centers of the Mics and the Macs. Then too, the initial attacks had very likely come suddenly, killing millions in the key cities of England. Other population centers, sufficiently warned, could have been evacuated.

"And so you want weapons," said Mark, gravely. "Anything else?"

Erlayok looked searchingly at him. Mark's face revealed nothing.

"Yes. There is one other thing," said the Earl, seriously. "As you can see, I am a man with a mentality far above the people around me. Now this benefactor of yours, Omega, has ambitions to populate the earth with a superior race. He has chosen you, and rightly, to carry out this purpose. Naturally then, it would further his purpose and yours, if I were also chosen to carry on my strain of genius. Am I not right?"

"I don't think so," Mark replied. "I wasn't chosen because of any streak of genius, for I have none. And besides, I have no knowledge of the way my blood is made. I couldn't give it to you if I wanted to. And I don't particularly want to."

Mark thought he saw the expression of unabated hardness come again to Erlayok's piglike eyes, but again it had passed too quickly for him to be certain.

"Then of course you could prevail upon this Omega to furnish it for me," he said, with assurance. "Such genius as mine should be allowed to survive more than the ordinary life-span. He will surely agree."

Once, Mark had met an oil magnate, an alumnus of his college. Fat, pompous, predatory. He had talked in much the same way of his enterprise and astuteness, terms which, frankly rendered, would have meant greed and rascality. Erlayok at least had more on the ball than that.

"I doubt if Omega will think you're quite the type," Mark said. "You see, Omega is not much impressed by any human intellect. Nothing our race has ever produced can compare with his own intelligence. He is only interested in good character traits. And he doesn't find many of them in humans. I don't think you'd get a very good report card on that score."

"But he is certain to recognize that I am superior to other humans," protested Erlayok. "And it is a superior race he proposes to start, so I must surely qualify."

Mark laughed. "Well, maybe. If you read my mind as thoroughly as you say, then you must know that a human with my type of blood requires no sleep. Twenty-four hours a day, his mind is active. Nor is his mind troubled by any physical disorders. The radio-active element in the blood not only heals wounds with lightning speed, but kills all disease germs. Therefore, the brain operates free of distractions of that sort.

"During the long nights when everyone else is asleep, he is awake. As a result he thinks, and thinks deeply. The average human never gets time to think. He is too busy making a living, or relaxing to build strength for the next period of work.

"Therefore, you see, the man with my sort of blood becomes a mental giant in time, even though he may have been only of mediocre intelligence in the beginning. So I don't think Omega would weigh your mental attainments very heavily. I, myself, will eventually surpass you. Right now I doubt that you could hypnotize me again. You caught me unaware the first time."

Erlayok laughed his offensive laugh. But Mark noticed that it had an uneasy note in it.

"WHY SHOULD I hypnotize you?" Erlayok asked. "Let us leave the matter of blood to your Omega. You can suggest it to him, when he appears again. Right now let us talk of the weapons we need to free our people of the terrible yoke of taxes which oppress them. I shall provide writing materials for you. My artisans can work from your designs."

The huge noble started to cross the room toward an elaborately carved escritoire.

"Don't trouble yourself," Mark advised. "I couldn't draw plans for a gun or a tank if I tried all day. In my former existence I dabbled in electricity and radio, but armament is out of my line. If you read my mind so clearly, you should know that."

Erlayok's face hardened. He became the man he had been when Mark was brought into the room. Inflexible, cruel and ruthless. "You lie!" he charged. "In your mind I saw all sorts of technical knowledge about guns."

"Then why didn't you record that knowledge in your own brain?" Mark taunted. "Or isn't your mind as powerful as you would have me believe?"

Erlayok took a step forward. Mark poised on the balls of his feet, his hands stretched as far apart as the chains would permit. Once those hands, encircled that fat neck it would be the end of Erlayok, chains or no chains. But the Earl stopped.

"Fool. You know that this age is ignorant of technical things. I could see the knowledge in your brain, but I couldn't translate it." He paused and the expression of hardness left his face. Once again he was the amiable fat man.

"But what are we arguing about? We are friends. In exchange for the knowledge I wish, you have my promise that when our enemies are conquered, the people will benefit immediately. How much better is the solution of removing the necessity for our great army, than the bloody revolution that you rebels are planning. Bloodshed which will accomplish nothing, for the army will still be necessary, and consequently the taxes."

Mark looking into the eyes of Erlayok, felt the logic of his arguments. In the friendly expression on the big man's face there was only an earnest desire to convince Mark of the truths that would lift the intolerable burden from his people.

Mark felt suddenly ashamed of his own cheap cynicism. Erlayok was so obviously interested in the welfare of the Brish, so little caring for his own personal gain. Why had not Mark seen this before? Such a man would not use a knowledge of deadly weapons for the purpose of conquest.

Even Nona had always accused him of being too wary and too suspicious. And she was right. Mark was convinced that in the face of his new opinion of Erlayok, he should reveal his knowledge of guns and tanks. First impressions should not be trusted. The plans for the guns....

Suddenly Mark remembered that he knew little of the actual designs of guns. And nothing of the chemical formula of gunpowder. He had shot guns; he was, in fact, an expert marksman. That was why Erlayok had thought he could build one.

ABRUPTLY A new thought struck home. He had just decided to design guns for this man, who was now such a fine fellow.

And yet he knew it was impossible for him to do it. That decision hadn't originated in his own brain!

With the realization he looked searchingly into the eyes of Erlayok. In them he sensed a bafflement, a sort of frustration. Erlayok was finding his subtle form of hypnotism running against a stone wall.

Mark felt a probing force beat against his brain, and the expression of the fat man changed to sudden bestial anger, mingled with a fierce determination.

The Earl was marshaling all his mental force to break down Mark's stubborn will. The waves of mental energy hammered and surged against Mark's brain. But he didn't lose consciousness as he had before. This time he was warned and prepared. He got angry and steeled himself.

The nerve of that pudgy ape tinkering around with the inside of his mind! Why, it was outright indecent. Mark was furious.

The mental suggestion of friendliness and virtuous intention was the sort of thing that could sneak up on him before he knew he was being hypnotized. But now that he was warned and alert, he was safe from the most powerful mental force. His brain, as well as his body, was automatically feeding itself upon the radiations of his peculiar blood, and was tireless.

He could maintain his resistance indefinitely, while Erlayok was tiring fast. Serve him right. Mark hoped he'd break a blood vessel. The hammering grew weaker and, finally stopped abruptly. The big man slumped in his chair, his eyes glazed.

"Satisfied?" Mark grinned. "I can't design guns because I haven't the knowledge. Even if you could break me down you couldn't get the answer."

Mark's voice served to revive the Earl. Life came into his eyes and he sat erect. Suddenly he picked up the decanter of wine and threw it directly at Mark. Speedy reflexes bobbed Mark's head out of its path and the glass decanter shattered against the door.

"There are more ways than one of breaking a man down," snarled Erlayok.

His face, twisted into a savage grimace, warned Mark of what might be in store for him. He strained to pull the chains apart. The decanter hadn't been tossed at him after all. Erlayok had known that he would duck and it would strike the door. The guards, who had retired no further than the other side of that door, would be summoned by the crash. And the Earl, gloating, could be planning only one thing. Torture.

The frantic tugging was useless. Before he could do more than stretch the tough links, the guards rushed in and pinned him.

"Now, my sanctimonious friend," Erlayok gloated, "we shall see whether or not you will speak. My torturers have something of genius in them, too. They have never failed. And if it will make you feel any better, I'll teach you this:

"When I equip my men with guns, I shall do more than drive the Mics and the Macs out of our land. I shall enslave them! And your people—your Vikes who consider themselves the world's greatest warriors; who refuse to dignify the might of the Brish by waging war, but merely raid us when they so desire—they shall pay for their arrogance. I'll descend upon them with every fighting man our ships will hold! I'll wipe them off the face of the earth!"

Mark glared defiantly. He knew the Earl would do none of these things. And his steady gaze did little to pacify the rage of Erlayok. The man was seething, his face working with the madness that gripped him, as he herded the party down the marble stairs toward the dungeons.

CHAPTER IX

THE FRIGHTENED TAILOR

THE GUARDS KEPT the razor-edged swords poised menacingly at Mark. If he was to have an opportunity to turn the tables on his captors, the time was certainly not now. The slightest move would find several of the swords sheathed in his body. And while he now knew of the miraculous healing powers of his blood, he certainly wasn't going to risk injury to vital organs.

The party didn't stop at the level of the dungeons, as he had expected. A stone door revealed a flight of steps going even lower.

A smelly oil lamp, carried by one of the guards, revealed a sight that caused Mark to feel a crawling horror. Here was a place that might have been transported bodily from an era, thousands of years past, when the good church fathers of Spain used terrible methods to extract confessions of heresy from unfortunates who were so foolish as to have incurred their enmity.

A charnel odor assailed his nostrils competing with the effluvium of the smoking oil lamp. Mark was oppressed by a feeling of unreality as he surveyed a conglomeration of the crudest instruments of torture ever conceived by twisted human minds.

Some of these contraptions were familiar, the sort which might be found in any age of any land where torture was a usual practice. Such things as thumb-screws, foot-crushers and racks were universal, evidently requiring little imagination to devise. But there were other instruments, some of them designed for unguessable purposes, that were obviously the products of some modern genius of this brutal age. Mark shuddered again.

THE SECRET cellar of Smid's haberdashery housed a serious conference. The night had passed, interminably long for the rebels gathered here. Murf had insisted that Mark would return, for he was confident that his superior strength and cunning would enable him to escape from his awkward position at the prison door. But Mark had not put in an appearance.

As the hours progressed and hope that he would return grew dimmer, Murf organized the men into an information gathering crew. Each man was given a separate line to follow in an effort to trace the disappearance of their leader. One of them was sure to uncover a lead.

Immediately after the ringing of curfew they sallied forth.

In a surprisingly short time two of the men returned, each with information. One of them, with a brother-in-law in the service of Erlayok, told of the terrible fight Mark had given the Earl's soldiers. He guessed that Mark was being held prisoner in Erlayok's palace.

The other, who insisted that his story was for Murf's ears alone, had even more.

His sister, it appeared, was a menial in the service of the Earl. Last night, he related, a bit shamefaced, she had not returned to her home, but had stayed in the palace. He suspected that she had a sweetheart among the guards. Her mother, who had worried about her, had presented herself at the palace gates immediately after curfew, to inquire of her daughter's where- abouts. The daughter was there, all right, and explained to her mother that she had been delayed in the palace until after the beginning of curfew. She gave the cause, in strictest confidence, as being the excitement due to the capture of the leader of the rebels.

Murf summoned Smid and told him the news, Smid's eyes widened in an ague of fear. Questioning by Erlayok meant only one thing. Mark would be tortured until he was forced to reveal the identities and whereabouts of every rebel he knew anything about. Smid had no belief in the fortitude of any man subjected to the Earl's diabolic attentions.

Murf, apparently, held the same idea. "We must stop it," he muttered. "Jon, Duke of Scarbor, is the answer!"

"But who shall seek his aid?"

"Who but myself?" asked Murf, starting for the stairs that would lead him to the street.

"But you can't!" Smid protested. "Think of the risk!"

"Think of the risk if I don't," retorted Murf. "All our work could be wrecked in less than a day. I'm going."

"But if Erlayok knew that Mark was connected with the rebellion, then he is sure to know you are. You practically started it. And he'll trace you back to here." As he said this, Smid's voice rose to a screech.

"Fool." Murf made a swipe at him with open hand, "If he knows me, then he already knows of this place. The point is that we must stop Erlayok from questioning Mark. Once I get inside, with the help of Jon, I can prevent it. If it was any other man, I wouldn't take the chance. But Mark knows all our hidden ramparts. He mustn't talk! Now, my friend, can you suggest anyone to take my place? If you can't, give peace to your puling tongue and let me go."

SMID WAS cuffed into silence. Nobody but the outrageous Murf would have the courage to enter the stronghold of the enemy. Only Murf, who had some driving urge to see the rebellion an accomplished fact—an urge that seemed far stronger than that of any of the other rebels, would have the audacity to do the awesome thing that was so necessary.

"You will make sure his lips are sealed?" Smid inquired, hesitantly, as Murf again started up the stairs. "You will remember our safety and not be weak?"

Murf paused, ran a thumb along the keen edge of his knife, and replaced it in his belt.

"If necessary," he muttered. "The cause is more important than any one man." There was a laughing light to his eyes as he spoke that made Smid's bony knees clack together in apprehension. Murf was either a wild fanatic or—or a very clever actor.

Smid watched him disappear in the direction of the palace of the Duke of Scarbor, and shook his head.

Smid remembered when he had harbored his first doubts as to Murf's sincerity, his first, uneasy suspicion that Murf might be an emissary of the Mics, who coveted the rich farm lands of the Brish. His red hair, and the fact that he had no past that anyone could trace, added fuel to these suspicions. His glib tongue, and his genius for organizing had served as sufficient reason for thinking that he was just the sort of man who would be sent by the Mics on such a mission. He had tried to trip Murf up, to no purpose. Never once had Murf slipped in his masquerade—if it really was one.

On the other side of the ledger was the fact that Murf had red hair, and Smid couldn't conceive of the Mics sending a man upon whom suspicion would so readily fall even at sight. And if he was an agent of the Mics, he would certainly be furnished with a very plausible background in the form of a carefully fabricated past. In addition, his zeal and willingness to take terrible risks in furthering the cause, were evidence in themselves to allay any doubts of the man's sincerity.

So Smid didn't know and he was unhappy. But then if he wasn't worried about Murf, he was harassed by fears of a possible rise in the price of cloth or by a deep-rooted foreboding that one day his shop would burn to the ground or by almost anything else that popped into his head. Smid saw disaster everywhere, and he knew it, and so he couldn't disentangle his suspicions of Murf from his apparently groundless terrors about everything else under the sun. It was all very distressing.

AT THE palace gates Murf demanded an audience with Jon. He demanded it in the name of Mark, the savior of the Duke's life. Had he used any other name, he might well have been kicked into the moat. But he knew that the story of the rescue was well known and would gain him admittance. The guardians of the gate were acquainted with the generosity of the Duke, and knew that he would be displeased if they sent Murf away. Accordingly the redhead was led inside.

Jon, Duke of Scarbor, was seated at breakfast with his wife. Without ceremony, Murf was brought into the room. Jon, recognizing him, waved a hand toward a chair at the table. Such democratic treatment surprised the redhead, but he dropped into the seat and dove into his story.

Jon slowly laid down his fork and wiped his fingertips. "But why, man?" he asked. "What can Erlayok want of him? He wouldn't imprison and torture a man without some reason."

"I don't know, Highness. I only know that this is true. Won't you intervene? Our laws, stringent as they are, still protect us from such things. Mark, if he is accused of a crime, is entitled to imprisonment in a public jail while awaiting trial."

Jon looked across the table toward his wife. Her eyes mirrored a sudden fright, but her words belied it. "You must, of course," she said, calmly. "Our decision has been made."

"You are quite right, my dear," he answered. "The gods favor our course."

The Duke stood erect and pushed back his chair. Clapping his hands, he summoned a guard and issued terse orders. A servant appeared with a black cape, which he buckled at his neck. In short minutes he and Murf were mounted and surrounded by armed horsemen of the guard. They galloped off in the direction of Erlayok's palace.

CHAPTER X

THE DUKE GOES TO TOWN

ENTRANCE TO THE grounds was easily accomplished. The men at the gates swung them wide at the sight of the Duke. But once inside they met delay after delay. No one seemed to know where Erlayok could be found. His servants displayed decided reluctance to talk. The Earl's quarters were deserted, they quickly discovered, and a guard at the gate told them that Erlayok had not left. But no servant or other person connected with the household would give any further information. They were all in abject fear of Erlayok's wrath.

"The dungeons!" said Murf. "These jackals are afraid to tell you that he has already started his horrible tortures." The r's of the adjective came rolling out like the chatter of the forgotten machine-gun.

But when the guard stationed in the gloomy corridor beneath

the palace allowed them to look in the cells, they found no trace of Mark.

"You have led us a merry chase," Jon accused. "What idiocy did you hope to work?"

"Believe me, Highness. Mark is somewhere in this palace. Find Erlayok and you'll find him."

The absence of the Earl was strange, thought Jon. Perhaps it would pay to find him before passing judgment on this excited scamp. With the idea of again going through the upper floors he led his men back to the stairs. They passed the stone door leading to the chamber below, again failing to see it in the semi-darkness which prevailed in the dungeon corridor.

Murf, almost at the rear of the party, caught a whiff of the odor of stale wood smoke, mingled with a fetid stench of putre-faction. He turned to locate its origin.

"Wait!" he cried. "I've found him!"

Behind the door were two of Erlayok's guards. They raised their swords to stop the intruders, and were forthwith struck down by the foremost of Jon's soldiers.

Stepping quickly past his men, the Duke entered the grim chamber. What he saw brought a sickly anger to the pit of his stomach. His eyes flashed a single gleam, then he straightened and spread his hands behind him to prevent the sudden rush of his soldiers into the room. The men gathered around Mark were so intent on what they were doing to him that they had not heard a sound.

Strapped tightly in a stone chair, Mark was glaring defiantly at his tormentors. With enormous deliberation, a man in the livery of Erlayok was pressing a white-hot iron against Mark's fleshy chest. While open wounds didn't bother Mark much, the searing heat of the iron was exquisite agony. And Mark couldn't let them know what they were doing to him. His flesh might be as good as invulnerable to the destructive, blasting touch of the metal, the delicate little nerves that transmitted the scourg-ing pain to his brain were not. But he had to make them go on thinking he was a wizard, insensible to mortal dolors, and so he kept his face a stiffened mask, and held the light of defiance in his gaze. He didn't see how he could keep the mask from shattering though when they rubbed salt on the place where the iron had been.

Each man bent closer to look at the ravaged flesh. A quick hiss of indrawn breaths. This was not the first time the iron had been applied. But when the man rubbed his hand across Mark's chest, the charred spot brushed away, leaving no sign of a burn! There was only a small spot, the size of the end of the iron, which was lighter in color than the sun-bronzed surrounding skin.

"The gods favor him!" said one of the soldiers with an awed voice. The others nodded.

Erlayok made a strangled sound as he tried to control his rage. "Fools!" he said. "The man is a demon, but I'll make him talk, just the same. His eyes won't heal like that, jab a hot iron in one of them!"

THE DUKE, himself astonished, nevertheless thought it time to interfere. He stepped into the room. Erlayok, seeing him out of the corner of an eye, turned, snarling.

"Explain this!" the Duke demanded.

Erlayok made a visible effort to control himself. It was an heroic task and he accomplished it. He almost achieved the genial expression he had worn a short while before. Almost, but not quite.

"I'm not in the habit of explaining anything which happens in the privacy of my own house. Perhaps you will explain your intrusion."

The Duke's face hardened. "It's useless to argue, Erlayok," he said. "In matters of policy you can overrule me with your control of the votes of the lesser nobles, but in matters of law I am still supreme magistrate in the Duchy of Scarbor. Why are you holding this man and subjecting him to torture?"

Erlayok hesitated, scratching his chin. Mark spoke up, before he could formulate an answer. "He's trying to make me tell him of some ancient weapons he thinks I can design for him. He wants to use them to conquer the Mics and the Macs and make them pay tribute to him."

"Nonsense," Erlayok said. "One of my men recognized him as being a member of the insurgent organization. We are trying to make him tell of his associates."

Jon looked at Murf, who didn't change expression.

"You can prove this?" he asked.

"Certainly! There among your party is another rebel. A little torture will make *him* talk." Erlayok pointed to Murf, who still remained impassive.

"We don't use such barbaric methods," said Jon, flatly. "If you have no evidence against the redhead, we can't even hold him. And two weeks ago I pardoned him of all former crimes. Have you evidence he has committed any since?"

Erlayok shook his head. "No," he said. "But this other man *can* be held. You have said you are chief magistrate. You can stand in judgment right now." He turned to two of the men among the torturers. "Tell the good Duke where we found this man. And when!"

The soldiers told of capturing Mark several hours after curfew, walking the city streets, not omitting the terrific battle it to subdue him. Erlayok smiled triumphantly at the Duke.

"He has had his trial now," Erlayok pointed out. "If he's guilty, then pass your sentence."

The Duke looked at Mark. "You have heard the testimony of these men. Do you wish to deny the charge?"

"No," said Mark, to the Duke's surprise. "I *was* walking the city streets after curfew." The sweat was still streaming from his pores and he was breathing jerkily through lungs that felt as thin as paper.

"But man!" the Duke exclaimed. "Don't you know the punishment for that offense?"

Mark nodded. "Drawing and quartering, I've heard. A fit punishment for such a hideous crime." His eyes accused Jon of being no less a barbarian than Erlayok, and Jon was suddenly uncomfortable. He had always tried to be a good man, yet here was a stranger who challenged him to be a better one than he knew how to be. And from somewhere inside, Jon found a deeper courage than he had ever thought he had.

The Duke shook his head sadly. "I didn't make such laws," he muttered, defending himself involuntarily. "It's only my job to enforce them." He paused, and a gleam came in his eyes. He surveyed the splendid physique of the bound man. "I have seen you in action," he said thoughtfully. "And I've listened to the story of your fight with Erlayok's men. And legally there is an alternative sentence I can impose."

This much he felt strong enough to do in defiance of Erlayok, whom he had always feared. But fear didn't stop him this time.

Jon paused again and smiled at the expression of anger that crossed the face of the Earl. "This is the third week of the harvest festivities. Tomorrow, and every day until Saturday, there will be games and exhibitions in the central arena. I sentence you to participate in them. Perhaps you may survive. It depends on you."

CHAPTER XI

OFF WITH HIS HEAD

MARK SMILED HIS thanks. He knew that Jon, in his generosity and gratitude, was doing all he could. As for himself, he hadn't feared the sentence of drawing and quartering. He still had confidence in his ability to escape before the sentence could be carried out. And with the knowledge that somewhere Nona was probably mourning him, it was his full intention to do so at the earliest moment. The rebellion would be an accomplished fact in a very few days after he put his forces in motion, and then he would be free to return to her.

With a roar, the sergeant
lunged out with his sword.
The move was ill advised

Erlayok motioned one of his men to unbind him. "Put him in one of the cells," he directed. "Under guard!"

"No," the duke interposed. "I shall see that he is adequately guarded. In a city prison."

For an instant it seemed that Erlayok would go completely berserk. His face twisted and his hands clenched and opened like the claws of some bird of prey. But abruptly he calmed and smiled, as if at some delightful secret. Mark, as he was led out of the chamber, wondered what charming thought was behind the smile.

At the palace gates the party remounted. One of Jon's soldiers gave his horse to Mark. Ordinarily a prisoner would have been forced to walk, but the Duke evidently didn't consider Mark a criminal.

Murf rode part way to the city prison, and then requested an opportunity to bid his friend goodbye, before going his way. The Duke, with a wry smile, ordered his men to draw away a short distance.

"You won't be in jail very long," Murf said, hurriedly. "I'll get our forces together as quickly as it can be done. We'll free you and begin the attack. Our men will fight all the better with the prospect of turning you loose to lead them."

"No," Mark said. "Wait a day or two, I'll break out of prison without any help. When we stage the attack it must be a complete surprise. And aimed only at the strategic points we have agreed upon. If our forces waste time storming a prison to free me, the nobles will have a chance to consolidate their available fighting men. The element of surprise may mean the difference between success and failure. Not to mention the difference in the number of men who must die."

Jon, aware that something other than an ordinary farewell was in progress, motioned his men to break up the conference.

"The horse is yours," he told Murf. "Don't use it for any dishonorable purpose."

The redhead grinned impishly and nodded his thanks. "I wish Your Highness, and Your Highness' family, a long life," he said, enigmatically. And with that he dug his heels into the horse's flanks and rode off, waving a hand.

"Quite decent of him," the Duke remarked, watching the disappearing figure.

THE PARTY continued down the winding streets, the horses' well-shod hooves a-clatter on the cobbles. They proceeded at the leisurely pace necessary because of the ox-carts and pedestrians that thronged the streets.

Several times there was cheering and shouting as the horsemen were recognized. Mark, riding beside Jon, thought the tribute was intended for the Duke as he saw the admiring and worshipful looks cast in his direction. Jon, he believed, was regarded by the people as being a man of gentler stamp from the nobles who oppressed them. They knew of his futile efforts to help their conditions, and loved him for trying.

"They like you," Jon observed ruefully. "I wonder what they would do if they knew I was taking you to jail."

Mark was astonished. "The cheers were yours, not mine."

"Some of them, perhaps," the Duke admitted. "I have been

cheered before, on the city streets. But never as much as today. So I'm not fooling myself." He smiled, almost wistfully. "I do envy you. I wish I—Never mind."

Mark insisted. "If any of these people are cheering me, they are doing it only because I once saved your life. And that, of course, is only a left-handed way of paying you tribute."

The Duke looked at Mark, his eyes twinkling. "I may be stupid but I am not entirely uninformed, my friend," he said.

Before Mark could puzzle out the meaning of this remark, the party arrived. Mark had been brought to the same jail from which he had so blithely escaped the night before. He hadn't known that this was the nearest public prison to the Earl's palace, and had assumed that he would be taken to some other place.

The massive door in the courtyard was wide open, and seated in the heat of the sun were the four guards, engaged in their eternal game of cards. They raised their heads as the Duke's party entered the yard and Mark instantly recognized one of them as the man who had summoned the soldiers. The man jumped to his feet, and after bowing formally to the Duke, blurted the story of the raid, pointing toward Mark as the guilty party.

But surprisingly, Jon was not perturbed at the news. He acted, in fact, as if the story were not news at all. He merely nodded and told the man, who, it appeared, was the sergeant of the guards, that Mark was already condemned to participate in the games. He added that the prisoner was not to be molested in any way, so that he would be in one piece to give the audience a good show.

The sergeant grinned. "How about food?" he asked. "The usual prison fare, or should I feed him well so he'll last longer in the arena?"

"Starve him," the Duke decided. "It'll make him all the more ferocious."

WITH ANOTHER grin, the sergeant herded Mark through the door and into a cell. Mark went quietly, resolving to tear the cell door off its hinges as soon as the man shut the inner portal of the guardroom. He was disagreeably surprised when he saw the other three men carrying their table and benches down the corridor. These they placed directly opposite his cell. Sunlight, coming through the window he and Murf had once used as a means of escape, struck the table top and furnished light for the game.

"You're our only prisoner," chortled the sergeant, "and we can give you all our attention. So just make yourself comfortable and meditate on the habits of certain fowls that always come home to roost." The sergeant's enormous belly shook as he laughed in appreciation of his own joke. Then he sobered. "And if you think you can walk out of here by bending those bars, just try it! We'll slice your fingers off at the elbow!" He laughed again and placed his sword within easy reach of his hand.

Mark, inwardly indignant, grinned as if everything was to his liking. This required quite a bit of thinking. He began to strip off the nightwatchman's rig he had been wearing since the night before, and carefully spread it on the dusty floor of the cell. Then he sat down on it and leaned his back against the wall.

One of the guards shivered beneath his warm leather jacket as he saw Mark's bare back touch the wall. The prisoner was now wearing nothing but a pair of sandals, recently acquired, and the skin tight trunks he had worn when he emerged from the ocean. His belt contained no weapons.

Mark felt a certain satisfaction as he noted the wondering expressions on the faces of the guards as they began their game. He was playing a game too. A waiting game.

There was, after all, no reason why he should escape immediately. There were only four men outside, and if he waited long enough there would be only two. They would eventually break up their game and take turns at sleeping. And when the first two went they would leave two drowsy comrades behind.

And if Mark pretended to be asleep at that time, maybe they would doze off. In fact, it was almost certain that they would.

As he silently watched the flicking cards and listened to the sound of clinking coppers, Mark's thoughts dwelt on the enigma of Jon, Duke of Scarbor.

He knew that the Duke was a right-minded man, sincerely trying to see that justice was done, and earnest in his attempted reforms. He knew also that the Duke was wholeheartedly supporting his subjects' desire for lighter taxes and elevation from serfdom. He also was aware that the Duke was a noble of royal blood and therefore could be expected to take sides with the nobles to quell any possible rebellion.

Yet Jon had gone to great lengths to defy Erlayok and release Mark. And he had also befriended Murf, a known insurgent. Gratitude alone failed to completely explain such actions.

Mark recalled the cheers which the Duke had insisted were for him. And his own clumsy effort to twist their meaning. The Duke had said, "I am not entirely uninformed." And had smiled when he said it.

That seemed to indicate that Jon was aware that Mark was the leader of the rebels. And the fact that he had turned Murf loose, and had even made him a present of the horse, might indicate that the Duke was in favor of a rebellion.

The idea was plausible. Jon had been balked in his own efforts to better conditions among his people. Perhaps he considered a rebellion was worthwhile if the desired end was gained.

The Duke had certainly been a friend when he'd barged into that torture chamber. Those burns had hurt, even if they hadn't done any lasting damage. And he had further shown his friendship when he had ordered Mark's guard not to damage him. Yet he had also told them to starve him. But he had smiled then, too.

Mark wondered about that. It didn't seem possible that the Duke could know that he didn't require food. Even Murf wasn't sure about that. Several times in Murf's presence he had eaten a mouthful or two. Mark hadn't told of his unique properties because of the involved explanation it would require. And with the limited knowledge of the day, the phenomenon would probably fall in the category of black magic, anyway.

A diversion at the card table distracted him.

FOR THE past few minutes he hadn't been watching the game very closely, though he did notice that the pile of copper coins at the sergeant's elbow was getting higher and higher. Suddenly the player opposite him sprang to his feet and threw his cards face up on the table. At the same instant the sergeant swept his hand back in a grab for his sword. But the other man was quicker. In a flash his sword was drawn and in action.

As the sergeant came erect with his own weapon swinging, he was probably very surprised to find that he had been decapitated.

At any rate, he took practically no interest in the proceedings from that point on. The head came to rest altogether too far away to concern itself with the welfare of the body, which slumped in utter dejection. His conqueror calmly cleaned his sword on the trousers of the vanquished.

"Tsk, tsk," Mark commented as he noted the cards on the table. There were five of them face-up, and all five were aces. He didn't know the nature of the game they had been playing, but he had observed that there were four suits in the deck. The dealer—and the sergeant had dealt this hand—had made a serious mistake.

The two other players were still too stupefied to do more than stare at the victor. That gentleman reached over and appropriated about one-third of the sergeant's winnings.

"I did you men a favor," he said. "That crook would have had the rest of your money if I hadn't done what I did. Now you do me a favor. Give me a good start out of here before you report this. And when you do report it, make it self-defense. That's what it was, you know. He went for his slicer first. But I'm not taking any chances. I'm joining Erlayok's army right now. They can't touch me if I do that. Erlayok takes care of his men. Now give me about fifteen minutes. Okay?"

The two nodded dumbly and the man wheeled and left. As soon as the outer door slammed they made a concerted dive for the remainder of the coppers. Then they proceeded to go through the pockets of the deceased, picking him clean.

Mark eyed them closely, missing nothing. For a moment he toyed with the idea of trying to bend the bars of his cell door while they were occupied. He decided to wait, however, realizing that he wouldn't be able to bend them far enough to slip through before they would be upon him, slashing his fingers with their knives.

And a frustrated attempt to escape now, would render them all the more alert later.

After dividing the loot, the two guards went into a conference. Then one of them left to notify the authorities what had happened. The other tilted a bench against the wall and sat facing Mark's cell, his sword in his hand.

Mark stayed quiet, but his mind was busily trying to see a way to turn these unforeseen events to his advantage. He only had one guard to contend with, but that wasn't much help. The man was wide-awake and alert. Mark knew that the keen-edged sword could slice his hands beyond the ability of his blood to repair, in the minute or two that would be required to bend the bars.

CHAPTER XII

THE SPINELESS SWORD

IN A FEW minutes the opportunity was lost anyway. The guard returned and brought several other men with him. One of these was garbed in a uniform unfamiliar to Mark. He carried no sword, merely an ornamented dagger in a sheath. The uniform was otherwise gaudy and Mark decided he was someone in authority. This man looked carefully at the arrangement of furniture, the position of the corpse. He even smiled when he saw the five aces. Finally he bent over and went through the pockets of the corpse. Then he frowned.

"There is no money on the body," he said, heavily.

Both guards burst forth in voluble explanation. Nothing could be made of the garbled sounds until the official silenced one of them with a wave of his hand.

"He didn't have any money in the first place," the other said. "We won all he had last night, fair and square. Then we lent him enough to get in the game today. So all he had was on the table and that belonged to us because he won it by cheating."

The official stroked his chin and nodded his head. "I'm glad you explained that," he said. "Robbing the dead is a serious offense. However your statement of the true circumstances will be accepted when I write it out and present it to my superiors. My time is valuable, of course, so I'll charge you each a fee of fifty coppers for writing it."

"But excellency!" one of the men exclaimed. "That is more than...."

The other one silenced him with a kick on the shins. With resignation they handed over the hundred coppers. The official smiled happily. He was faring better than as if he had robbed the corpse himself.

The transaction completed, his men went about removing the body. One of them tucked the head under his arm, facing to the rear as he went down the corridor. The two guards almost jumped out of their skins as the head leered at them before it disappeared through the door. Mark failed to see this little incongruity or he might have had some warning of what was to happen shortly.

As it was he had dismissed the matter of the slaughtered guard from his mind. If the two missing guards were replaced before the day was over, he was no better off than before. If they weren't, his position was improved to the extent that when the time came for one of the remaining two to sleep, he would be guarded by only one drowsy man.

For some reason Mark wasn't in any great hurry to escape. When he did break out, Murf would insist on making the first surprise moves in their planned rebellion immediately. True, Mark had agreed that now, in the disorganization of the holiday festivals, was the most propitious time to strike. And certainly the rebellious factions were now united as strongly as they ever would be.

But perversely, and in spite of the enthusiasm he had shown for the past weeks in his campaign, he was hesitant about putting forces in motion which would certainly result in great bloodshed.

HIS MIND went back to the stories he had read of the French Revolution. Of the thousands of innocent heads that had been lopped off. He remembered hearing first-hand accounts of the Russian Revolution. Of the bestiality that resulted, and of the savage destruction of irreplaceable works of art. Neither of these rebellions had resulted in any immediate improvement in the living conditions of the common people.

They had merely swapped one set of ruthless leaders for another, just as bad.

Might not this rebellion he planned get out of his control and wind up the same way? The ever-present menace of the Mics and the Macs could furnish the means. There would be temporary disorganization in the armies of the Brish, and during that time the country might be invaded and hopelessly subjugated. He hated to take the responsibility of starting something which might end so disastrously.

And the rebellion might well be a failure. His men could never hope to defeat the armies of the various nobles. And if the surprise element of his attack should fail of its purpose, they would surely have to contend with those armed forces. They would be slaughtered without mercy.

Only by simultaneously defeating the garrisons of all the nobles could they hope to succeed. For this would automatically give them control of the armies. The palaces of the various earls contained the vaults which held the vast sums collected as taxes and land rentals. And from these vaults came the money to pay the salaries of the soldiers.

If the rebels took these strongholds, the allegiance of the armies was assured. But if they failed, those soldiers would hunt them down and kill them.

And even if they won and escaped attack from their hereditary enemies, would conditions be very greatly improved?

For the first time Mark began to have doubts even of this. The tremendous armies would still have to be maintained. Forces for control of civil affairs would still be necessary. Crime would still require curbing.

Of course, there would be a great improvement in criminal procedure. And the army would no longer be allowed to ride roughshod over the rights of the citizens. There would be fewer injustices and inhumanities committed.

But would these things be worth the bloodshed that was inevitable, or the disastrous possibilities which must be risked?

The rebels expected much good to result from their victory. They were going to be bitterly disappointed to learn that taxes would still remain at a high level, so high that they would still be required to work from dawn to dusk to pay them.

Erlayok had pointed out that the only economies which could be safely effected would be to remove the expense of supporting the ruling class in luxury. And that there would still have to be rulers to support. The amount which could be saved would be relatively small. And it wouldn't satisfy the rebels, he could foresee.

His attention returned to the guards. Those two, quite oblivious to the recent decapitation of the sergeant, were now hotly engaged in a two-handed game. The stacks of coppers were about evenly matched. Evidently neither was winning. They were seated at the ends of the table so that both could see the prisoner. Both, furthermore, were chewing cuds of tobacco, and using Mark's cell for a cuspidor. They seemed to take great pride in their ability to spit between the bars. Mark himself appeared to be out of range, but he didn't regard the sport with any great favor.

THE GUARD on the left pushed forth a coin and laid his cards face down.

He was raising a bet. But he was too busy with his tobacco juice to call it. The other player matched his coin and raised again. The man on the left took another peek at his hand and decided to call. As he put one coin in the center of the table he raised his head and puckered his lips in the direction of Mark's cell. It looked to the prisoner as if a distance record were being contemplated and he prepared to pull his feet out of range.

Surprisingly, the ejected stream didn't so much as reach the door of the cell. Instead it curved in mid-air, as if driven back by a sudden gust of wind, and returned to splash full in the spitter's face. The other guard was convulsed with laughter and Mark mumbled: "Serves the blighter right."

The guard's laughter died suddenly and his face registered the unaccustomed impact of a thought. "Say—there—there wasn't any wind. How—"

The other one glared balefully at Mark, who smiled back sweetly. *"He* did it! He must have blew it back at me. I'll cut his heart out!"

Cursing handsomely, he reached for his sword. The other guard objected, warning him of the Duke's explicit order that the captive not be harmed.

"You better leave him alone. Don't know as I blame the poor guy anyhow. Jeepers, what lungs!"

The game went on.

But not for long, however. The corridor suddenly became the Cave of Winds. The cards developed a frisky will of their own. Apparently wafted by inexplicable gusts of wind, they would turn jauntily over and lie face up. They would drift off the table altogether and lodge in unprobable locations. Twice the man on the left carefully spat upon the floor, only to have sudden currents of air carry the brown spittle against his legs.

The guard on the right, whose cards behaved more capriciously, got so nervous about it that he would snatch them up the instant they were dealt.

The game finally broke up when he managed to get hold of three kings and a pair of queens, only to have them snatched out of his hand by a gust of unusual violence and deposited, with the pictures uppermost, in the center of the table. He swore loudly and with emphasis, glaring toward Mark's cell.

Strangely, both guards blamed it all on Mark. There was no reason for doing so, for the gusts had come from all directions and they could see that Mark hadn't changed his position. Possibly it was the fact that the prisoner saw nothing unusual in the peculiar antics of the wind. Perhaps it was because he was either grinning or laughing at them all the time these things were happening. But whatever the reason, they glared at Mark every time anything unusual occurred. And in a sense they were right. The peculiar happenings were directly due to his presence. Without him, nothing strange would have occurred.

THEY COULDN'T hear him chortling to himself: "Omega, you old reprobate. Give 'em the works—and then get me out of this cross-barred spittoon." They couldn't know about Mark's familiar spirit, whose unmistakable signature was scrawled all over the antics of the cards.

One of the guards grasped his sword and lunged menacingly at Mark's cell door. "Now cut it, you!" he roared. Then his face puckered plaintively, "Gorm, we ain't doing you any harm."

Mark grinned at him and said nothing. Suddenly the blade of the guard's sword began to flop back and forth like an eel trying to escape. From a rigid length of gleaming steel it became a writhing object with the consistency of wet spaghetti. In horror, the guard flung it to the floor. It landed, flopped a few times like a fish out of water, and then lay still.

This latest foible seemed to take some of the spirit out of the guards. When a man's weapons can no longer be relied upon, he loses some of his assurance.

The guards placed little reliance upon the bars of the prison to hold their man. They had already inspected the bent bars of a cell further down the corridor. Nor did they feel much confidence in their own ability to stop a man of such vigor. Their mastery of the situation depended wholly upon their ability to use their swords to attack Mark's hands if he tried to bend those bars.

"How did you do *that?*" said one of them querulously.

"A trade secret," Mark confided. "Didn't they tell you I was a master of Black Magic?"

"No," said one, awed.

"Well, I am," Mark declared flatly, ignoring the whisper "Liar!" that drifted to his ears.

"Rats!" the other said. "There ain't no such thing!"

Mark smiled in a friendly manner. "Oh, but there is," he insisted. "Do you want me to prove it? Well then, spit. Anywhere at all. I leave the choice to you."

The guard paled, then rallied. "I *thought* you did that," he said. "But it's some kind of a trick. And you're not going to get out of that cell with any trick."

"Black Magic or trick, what's the difference?" Mark asked. "I'll walk out of this cell whenever I care to."

As he spoke, Mark waved a hand past his face to dislodge a fly which had decided to park on his nose. But the gesture seemed fraught with significance to the two guards. For at the same time they were astounded to see the door of the cell becoming a cherry-red color.

They stepped back, shaken, and so doing, one of them stumbled over a bench and landed in a heap. He didn't take his eyes off the door, however.

The bars lightened from red to a brilliant white, and to the accompaniment of angry crackling, melted and dripped in a pool on the stone floor.

Mark, at the back of the cell, felt the blast of heat that was released, and grinned. Omega was playing his favorite game. He loved to astonish ignorant humans with a display of his mastery of natural forces. The guards were properly impressed. They cowered against the far side of the corridor, evidently too scared to run from the heat which was singeing their hair.

"You see it would be simple for me to escape if I wanted," Mark said. "So you needn't keep such a close watch over me. Suppose you both run along now and continue your card game in your own quarters. I'm tired of looking at you. And I'm tired of having you spit in my cell."

The guard who doubted the existence of Black Magic suddenly experienced a return of his courage. "No," he shouted, brandishing his sword. But abruptly the weapon began to weave through the air like demented sea weed. The guard howled and let it go. Whereupon the sword drifted feather-light to the floor.

"Short memory," Mark observed. "Now you two do as I say, before I get mad. Don't worry about me. I'll be here for quite a while. Shoo!"

Mark made a violent gesture with the last word, and the guards fell over each other in their flight. Once in the outer room they slammed the door to the cell block and shot the bolts. And with the sound, Omega materialized in the familiar form of the wrinkled old man.

CHAPTER XIII

UNCLE OMEGA

MARK SAID FURIOUSLY: "It's about time you showed up. I've been having the darnedest time, and it's certainly no fault of yours I've come through so far in one piece. How's Nona?"

"She's okay," Omega assured him. "When I left her, the ship was within a hundred miles of Stadtland. She was madder'n a skinned wildcat because I wouldn't bring her here. And it's high time you learned to mind your manners, you young ingrate! How's your head?"

"All right," Mark said. "And I'm certainly relieved that for once you showed sense enough to keep Nona out of this. This is no place for a woman—even Nona. Gosh, now I miss that baggage. Nobody's really bawled me out in a month."

"Yeah," Omega agreed, eyeing Mark and rubbing his chin thoughtfully. "You do need taking down a peg. Too big for your boots."

Mark didn't like the look in Omega's momentarily borrowed sage's eyes. "Now, look here—" he began in alarm. The old man had gently vanished. "Come back here! you shyster. This is no time for—" His speech broke off in a short, indignant yelp as a large gray rat, appearing out of the wall, scampered unpleasantly across his face.

"Cut it out!" Mark roared and took a swipe at the skittering rodent. His knuckles banged first air, and then the wall. It was very painful. Mark cursed.

Mocking laughter echoed out of space. Mark jeered: "Behave yourself. Orson Welles did that hollow mirth stuff a heck of a lot better, and anyhow—"

But Omega was having much too good a time to stop so soon. His next divertissement was to turn into several pairs of disconnected hands that floated menacingly about in front of Mark's face. In spite of himself, Mark shivered and then drew in a deep breath as the hands, like a flock of gulls suddenly assembled for concerted attack upon an unwary fish, dove for his naked and defenseless stomach.

"Quit it, you playboy idiot!" was all Mark had time for before the hands descended upon him, fingers curved and outspread, and began to tickle as hard and as fast as they could. It was an expert job and a skilled masseur could scarcely have been more personal. To Mark, it was sheer torture. He was helpless, doubled up, and screaming with agonized and involuntary laughter.

When the hands retreated, Mark collapsed, winded.

"Say uncle," a voice commanded.

"I'll be—darned—if I—will," Mark panted, thoroughly annoyed. "I'll—get you—for that."

"All right," said the voice. "Here you go. Oops-a-daisy."

The hands swooped down, grasped Mark by his armpits and raised him swiftly to the ceiling.

"Put me down!" Mark demanded.

IN ANSWER, the hands let him down with terrifying speed, arresting his plunge inches above the floor with a suddenness that did things to his stomach that hadn't been done to it since he had last ridden in an office-building elevator, eight thousand years ago. But the good old sensation was still there, and Mark howled in angry protest.

"Say uncle," the voice repeated.

Mark clamped his lips together; and the hands, this time in no mood for fooling, dragged him through the air in a series of breathtaking loops and swirls that would have made a twentieth-century stunt pilot weak with admiration. It was remarkable what intricate maneuvers could be accomplished in such a limited space. And a man may be stubborn, but his sense of equilibrium, when properly outraged, will betray him at last.

"All right," Mark gasped weakly, wincing as the floor came up to bat him in the face for the twentieth time. "I surrender. And I love you very much, Uncle Omega—but for cat's sake, *put me down!*"

Mark came to a gentle rest on the floor, where he lay, eyes closed and gasping for breath, until his head and his eyes and the pit of his stomach began to function in something like unison again. He opened his eyes and was relieved to find Omega back in his old man's guise, sitting placidly in the corner.

Omega stirred. "That ought, to teach you," he said smugly. "And now let's get down to brass tacks. What are you doing here? When I looked in on you the other day you were making speeches to a bunch of misguided insurgents."

"Why didn't you say hello?" Mark inquired.

"You were busy and I had to get back and tell Nona I'd found you. She was worried sick. I told her not to expect you for a while. I knew you'd want to finish this job even after you regained your memory. You've got a fine knack for sticking your nose into things which don't concern you at all."

Mark made a rude noise. "What do you mean, don't concern me? You fixed things so that this peculiar body chemistry of mine is to be perpetuated. For which you have my gratitude, incidentally. A lifetime several thousands of years long would be monotonous without company of the right sort. But the very fact that you gave Nona my kind of a body chemistry, makes me extremely interested in the sort of a world my future descendants will have. Therefore, I'm starting a campaign for betterment, right now."

"And how are you going about it?"

"I'm not so sure any more," Mark confessed, with unaccustomed hesitation.

"Then suppose you answer the question I asked," Omega suggested. "I could get the information direct from your mind, you know. Only I don't do that to people I like."

"You mean how I happen to be in prison?"

"Yeah. Were you jay-walking?"

"Something about as serious." Mark went on to explain his encounter with Erlayok.

"Nasty character," Omega said. "I looked him over several years ago. Unmitigated scoundrel—and a tyrant."

"A genius, though," said Mark.

Omega caused his seamed face to take on an expression of surprise. "Who said so?" he demanded. "Your own intelligence is better than his by a long shot. Even if you behave like a looney."

"How do you figure that out?" Mark inquired. "He was able to hypnotize me before I knew what was happening."

"Doesn't mean a thing."

"Why not?" asked Mark.

"**LOOK AT** it this way," said Omega. "Back in your youth there was a powerful intellect known as Einstein. And as far as I know he had no hypnotic power at all. Whereas there were any number of mediocre intellects in the form of fakirs and magicians who had considerable talent in that field. Obviously then, hypnotic power has little bearing on the intelligence of the mind which uses it."

"Sounds reasonable," Mark conceded. "It never occurred to me, that there wasn't a direct relationship between the two."

"There isn't," Omega said. "Hypnotic power is merely a special ability of certain brains. It bears about the same relationship to intelligence as other special abilities, such as adeptness with figures. If you'll remember, there were men in your time who could add long columns of numbers with lightning rapidity. What did they do for a living? Were they great statesmen, mathematicians or erudite scholars?"

Mark smiled as he recalled several such cases. "There was one who worked behind the counter of a grocery store," he remembered. "If you ask me it takes a high grade of intelligence to sell anything to a woman who doesn't know what she wants. That is, without going stark raving mad in the process. Were you ever in a grocery store, my old one?"

"Yeah. I was in a trolley car once, too," Omega confided. "That was a lot of fun. A woman, who for some reason was carting around about a hundred pounds of excess weight, was trying to find a nickel among a mass of gadgets jumbled inside her handbag. These jiggers, I understood, were mainly aids to beauty, and all had some specific purpose. Not being a human, I don't have a very well developed appreciation of human pulchritude, but in my opinion this particular lady was fooling herself.

"But as I started to say, there was a long line of people waiting to get on the trolley, while she fumbled. The motorman was looking at his watch and breaking out in a cold sweat. Several passengers were evidently late for work. She finally found the nickel, and was quite surprised to see it turn into a slimy worm in her hand. The conductor, who had meanwhile managed to become an overgrown rooster, pecked at it hungrily. The lady left the car with several blood-curdling screams, much to the surprise of the other passengers, who hadn't noticed anything unusual."

Mark listened patiently to the reminiscence, resigned to the fact that anybody as old as Omega certainly had a right to become garrulous about past adventures.

"About hypnotism," he said. "I'm afraid I got off the subject, just what is hypnotism?"

"I think you did," Omega agreed. "Bad sign—indication of advancing age. Hypnosis may be said to be a condition in which the subject is in an exaggerated state of passive attention to some person or object. In that state he is very amenable to suggestion. He can be made to do all sorts of things. The hypnotist, also by suggestion, can make him imagine he is being subjected to any sort of environment. It might be a sultry July day, but if the hypnotist tells the subject that he has been deposited on an ice floe adjacent to the North Pole, he will shiver and turn blue from the cold."

"I know all that," said Mark. "I've experienced it from the viewpoint of the subject. But what causes it? How does the hypnotist get his subject into this condition?"

"Oh, so you want to be a hypnotist!"

"No," Mark denied. "I just got an idea, a little while ago. An idea of how I might make this little rebellion of ours pay the sort of dividends the rebels think it will."

"That's fine," Omega applauded. "Tell me about it."

"After you tell me what causes hypnotism."

"GETTING STUBBORN again, eh? Whenever you get an idea, it's such a momentous occasion that you want to enjoy it all by yourself. I've a notion to leave you to your own devices. Then where will you be?" Omega twisted the wrinkled old face into an expression of extreme malevolence. But Mark knew he didn't mean it, so he just grinned.

Omega finally relented. "All right, I'll tell you. The force which enables the hypnotist to subdue the will of the subject is a variety of thought wave. Thought, as you should know, is a wave which ranges among the shortest of the vibratory scale. Hypnotism is at the longer end of the thought range.

"You have an analogy in light waves. As you know, there are several distinct waves in the range which we call *light*. At the shorter end are the violet and ultraviolet. At the longer end are the red and infra-red, known as heat waves. In the thought range are also several distinct vibrations, with varying characteristics.

"At the lower end of the thought ranges is the one which I employ frequently. It enables the user to manipulate the forces of nature as he wishes. With it he controls those energies which pervade all space. He can change energy into matter, or matter into energy, in any combination he wishes. One of the simplest manifestations of this is the lifting or moving of bodies of matter by causing this universal energy to do the work. You have heard of humans who had this power, though none of them actually knew what he was doing, It is called *telekinesis*. But of course no human who ever possessed the power had enough intelligence to use it for any but the simplest of exercises. Almost invariably they would set themselves up as having supernatural powers, and astound people with exhibitions of chair lifting and table shaking.

"Slightly longer thought waves can be projected. This is called *telepathy*. Further along the range of thought is the wide band which controls the movement of animal bodies. These waves are common to all forms of life, however unintelligent. They carry the motor and sensory messages to and from the brain, and may be either voluntary or involuntary. These require a medium, such as nerve tissue, for their passage.

"Toward the longer end of the range we have the waves which enable humans to reason logically. They possess pretty well developed ability in this division, compared to the lower animals. And longest of all the thought waves is that of hypnotism. It appears in humans occasionally, though seldom to any great degree.

"Most hypnotists among humans have found it necessary to have the subject concentrate on some bright or rhythmically moving object to subdue him. Here, the subject is using his own limited powers to hypnotize himself. Erlayok is an exception in that he needs only the subject to concentrate momentarily on his eyes. His own power does the rest. Everything clear?"

Mark thought for a moment. "Why do some have it and others not?"

"For the same reason that some people can hear lower notes than others. And for the same reason that bats can hear notes totally outside the range of human hearing. The sensory organ involved is tuned a bit sharper. It's the same with this hypnosis business. Erlayok was born with thought apparatus of slightly wider range in one direction. Use and practice have made it powerful.

"You, yourself, have the same property. But the fact that you don't know how to use it has caused it to remain undeveloped. The same goes for telekinesis. If you knew how, you could develop the power of your brain to equal mine.

"You could create matter from energy! You could move mountains! But you don't know how to use consciously any but a small band of the thought range you possess. You can use only the third and fourth waves in the series. The motor and sensory waves which all animals use, and the reasoning band common to humans. You have good control of the latter, because of constant practice during the nights when other humans have to sleep."

MARK NODDED gravely. "You mean that these mental powers are there to the same extent that the unused muscles of my feet are present. I've never learned to pick up objects with my toes, but the muscles and nerves are there just the same. Some people know how to use them, but most don't."

"Correct," Omega agreed. "Some people can wiggle their ears independently. Others can make ridges in their scalps. These muscles are present in all humans, but very few know how to control them. As far as that goes, only a few people ever make any great use of the third division of thought waves. As you are well aware, most people don't know how to think. Any effort along those lines gives them a headache. Maybe it's just as well, though. There'd be an awful high suicide rate if humans once began to realize what futile sort of beings they are."

"Phooey!" said Mark. "But you've told me what I want to know. There is a way to make this rebellion result in sufficient good to warrant the bloodshed."

"Getting back to that idea, eh?"

"You know, we humans are not quite the primitive savages you would imply. We construct mechanical aids for our limited senses. We make instruments which can detect ultra-violet and infra-red. And other machines which manufacture them. The same goes for the sounds which our ears can't detect."

"That was thousands of years ago," Omega reminded. "Humanity has fallen back a long way since then. Man has his hands full feeding himself, now."

"The people of the Moon are worse off than that," Mark countered. "They're dead! Except for one unfortunate survivor."

Omega nodded with unaccustomed gravity. "I get your point," he admitted. "You mean that while my race is dead, with the exception of one representative of high attainment, your race, even though at low ebb at present, has possibilities of becoming great. Greater than I. Consider me properly squelched."

"Check," Mark said. "It will be millions of years before the earth will produce an intelligence equal to yours. But the fact remains that the human form of life has a certain indomitable spirit which can overcome all its shortcomings, if given time. It lags at times, and seems to have been lost, but always forgets errors and sets itself a new goal."

"Admitted," said Omega. "That's why I've taken steps to see

that the race does continue. But what's that got to do with your idea?"

"Nothing except that mankind's past efforts to supplement his senses mechanically have shown me that it should be equally possible to duplicate the waves of thought, especially those of hypnotism. Before I submitted to Doc Kelso's new anaesthetic, I used to spend most of my time fooling with radio and other wave equipment. I know a little something about it.

"**NOW SUPPOSE** I should design a machine which would project a beam of thought waves in the range of hypnotism. Suppose this beam extended in a straight line for several hundreds of miles, and transmitted the suggestion that danger was present in the vicinity. Anyone approaching the line of the beam would be suddenly stricken by a surge of man's strongest emotion, fear. And the closer a person came to the beam, the stronger would be the emotion. That person would have to turn back!"

"It could be done, I suppose," Omega admitted. "But what good would it do?"

"Well," said Mark, "suppose I placed the transmitter so that the beam extended along the border to the country controlled by the Mics. And another one along the northern border of England. And a few more along the coastline."

"Maybe you got something, son," Omega said. "It would prevent any fighting along all those beams. The Brish could not be invaded from any direction."

"Nor could the Brish invade," Mark added. "It would allow them to disband their armies safely. The men thus liberated would seek other forms of employment and thus shorten the working hours of everyone. There would be that many more producers, with no need for added production. The taxes would come down and money could be spent for useful purposes."

"Utopia!" said Omega. "But that would leave the country isolated. Nobody could get out."

"I'd leave gaps in the beam for shipping. They would be small and easily defended."

Omega was enthusiastic. "Splendid!" he exclaimed. "Half of mankind's troubles abolished in one fell swoop. What's holding you up? Get started!"

Mark spread his hands and smiled. "I need help," he confessed. "*Your* help."

"But what could I do for the colossal intellect that can bust out with an idea like that?"

"Don't be a worm. You know perfectly well I need to know the exact wave length and frequency of the hypnotic vibration. And I need instruments and tools. Unless you can create the desired projector—"

"I'm afraid not," Omega said, all seriousness now. "You see I have no flair for things mechanical. Without trying to run down your ability, mechanisms are primitive. For millennia I have been making the things I need directly from the raw energies which are available everywhere. Or converting those energies to any purpose I might have. But for me to work with a machine such as you propose would be as hard as for you to make fire with a pointed stick. But I can make tools and equipment for you to experiment with. I used to spend a lot of time in the old General Electric and Westinghouse laboratories, and I know what they look like."

"Fair enough," said Mark. "I'll need a lot of stuff. And there isn't much time. Tomorrow the games start. I'm going to fight in them, you know. Duke Jon's idea."

"What do you want to bother with that for? You can walk out of here right now, and put all your time on this business until you get it finished."

"Won't do," Mark snapped. "If I go back to rebel headquarters, Murf and the rest of them will want to start the rebellion right away. And if I disappear, the whole thing will fall through. There would be no use protecting the country with my idea, if

I leave the nobles in power. They'd just put the armies on boats and start wars of conquest.

"The only thing I can do is show up each day at the games, and work here in the prison the rest of the time. As long as my friends, the rebels, know that I'm alive, they'll wait for me."

CHAPTER XIV

THE IDES OF MARK

IT WAS FORTUNATE that the prison had been emptied on the night previous. As a result Mark and Omega had plenty of room to work in. Omega, his memory of the instruments and machines he had seen as faultless as if he had been working from blueprints, constructed devices in use during Mark's earlier life, almost as quickly as Mark could describe them.

Before long the cell block looked more like an electrical laboratory than part of a prison. The two guards remained timidly in the outer room, playing a desultory game of cards and staring moodily at the door to the prison.

When Mark had assembled all the things he needed to begin work, he suddenly snapped his fingers and made an exclamation of dismay. "Power!" he exclaimed. "I have batteries enough to conduct experiments, but once I manage to project the proper wave length I'm going to need a lot more than batteries can give. Or, in fact, more than I can get from any compact means I'm familiar with."

"Don't worry about power until you manage to design a transmitter for the hypnotic wave," Omega advised. "Once you have a machine for making that wave you will have all the power you can use."

"Just how do you figure that?"

"I already told you that hypnosis is a wave only slightly separated in frequency from the one which controls the energies of space. They're both waves of the same band-thought. Consider the analogy of sound waves. If you design a machine to produce the sound known as 'G,' you ought to be able to adjust the same device to produce 'A'."

Mark's eyes popped. "You mean it lies within the mechanical genius of man to produce a machine which could create matter from energy?"

"Why not? I remember one race of reasoning animals, no more intelligent than humans, who managed to supply all their power that way. The inventor was one who was gifted with the ability to use, to a small extent, the telekinetic power of his own brain. He determined the wave-length and duplicated it by machinery.

"The outfit wasn't nearly as versatile as a brain, but it was compact and easily constructed. Used universally, it supplied all the power needs of his people. Unfortunately the race was snuffed out thousands of years ago by an unexpected nova. Their planet was completely destroyed. And there were no survivors, because they were all on it. They hadn't managed as yet to utilize telekinesis for space travel."

"Too bad," said Mark. "But if they did it, humans can do it."

"Sure. But don't get cocky. It would be a lot better to aspire to the ability to do those things mentally. Mechanical perfection only leads to degeneration. Once a machine will do a thing for you, you no longer try to prove your own ability along the same lines. Did you ever see the fellow who used to pound on an adding machine? Do you think he would have made any attempt to improve his own ability to add or multiply? Of course not. The machine could beat him every time. So it would be silly.

"But for our present purpose all that will be needed, once you figure how to produce a wave as short as thought, is to adjust the machine to transmute spacial energy into the required amount of electrical energy. It should be simple."

Mark screwed up his face as he tried to think of a certain little point which had popped into his head as Omega talked and had popped right out again.

He gave it up and frowned at the darkness of the corridor. The sun, he noticed, had ceased to shine through the window. It had changed its position as the day wore on. He mentioned that he would need light to work by. Omega, with appropriate mystic wavings of the hands, changed the chemical structure of the surface materials of the walls and ceiling so that they emitted a soft glow, making the corridor as light as Mark could wish.

"Cold light," Omega explained, airily. "The same principle as the light contained in the end of a firefly. Your scientists were working on it, but they never quite got it."

MARK WORKED feverishly the whole afternoon. He had all the equipment he could possibly use and he had a dozen ideas as to how he might manufacture the desired wave. Each of these ideas had to be tried, and the task involved a terrific amount of labor.

Coils, inductances, vacuum tubes, and a myriad of other devices had to be set up and wired for each experiment. Omega had told him the exact properties of the waves and how it should be impressed to deliver a constant message of danger when picked up by a human mind.

Aside from the mere postulate, Omega wasn't a great deal of help. He offered a host of suggestions, most of which Mark vetoed impatiently.

Sometimes he would look at the apparatus Mark was hooking up, and shake his head, unable to follow the intricacies presented by the vibratory changes in progress in the various devices. Here was an endeavor in which Mark's intellect outshone that of the almost omnipotent Omega. The devising of instruments to aid his weak body and limited senses was man's forte, while Omega needed no such aptitude. His was the direct method of twisting the forces of nature with his mind, without the circumlocution of cumbersome mechanical devices.

Finally Omega, deciding that he was more hindrance than

help, went into the guard room and amused himself by annoying the guards. Presently two new men appeared, one of them a sergeant, to replace the missing two. Omega went back to Mark.

"You can keep them occupied as you did the others, can't you?" Mark said.

"Sure, but their coming made me think of something. You said you were going to participate in the games. Suppose after you get through entertaining the crowd tomorrow, the authorities decide to keep you in some other prison? There is one closer to the arena than this one. And I can't spend all my time watching over you. I have several things which require attention, off and on."

"What do you suggest?

Omega walked his decrepit body over to the spot where Mark was bending over an unfinished hook-up. Mark looked up and felt the impact of the ancient one's eyes. For an instant his senses reeled, and then he felt normal again.

"What did you do?" he asked, startled.

Omega grinned, toothlessly. "It just occurred to me that if you possessed about ten times the hypnotic power of Erlayok you could suggest to your captors, without them even suspecting it, that it would be safer to return you to this empty prison where four guards could take turns watching you."

"No doubt," Mark admitted. "But I don't get it. I haven't any hypnotic power at all."

"I told you that all humans have the brain structure necessary to generate the waves. But only a very few ever learn how to use them. The portions of the brain which could be so used remain undeveloped in the others. The same applies to telekinesis and telepathy. Why even your own scientists recognized the fact that only about two-fifths of the human brain was ever used. What the other three-fifths was for they they didn't know.

"And if you had learned to exercise, early in life, that portion which emits hypnotic waves, it would be pretty well developed by now. About ten times as well developed as the same portion of Erloyak's brain. So I just developed it for you!"

MARK LOOKED unconvinced. "But… I don't feel any different." He stopped and puckered his brows in concentration. "You forgot something," he finally said. "I still don't know how to use it, even if you did alter the structure of that portion of my brain. It's like a big muscle without any nerves to operate it."

Omega crouched down until his eyes were on a level with Mark's. Suddenly Mark felt an almost irresistible desire to go to sleep. But knowing that sleep was one thing he didn't have any need for, he automatically fought against it. And as he fought, he tried to create a similar suggestion in the mind of Omega. A futile gesture, of course, for the mighty mind of Omega could not be downed. But the effort gave Mark his first practice in the use of his new faculty. He was like a fledgling trying its wings; a boy boxing with his father and learning to coördinate hand and eye.

"Now," Omega finally said, "suppose you command the two new guards to come in here."

Mark considered the problem. It was very likely that the guards he had chased out of the corridor would try to prevent the new ones from coming back here. They wouldn't want the replacements to know that their prisoner had the jail under his control, even if they weren't the sort to try to spare these new men from an experience such as they had undergone. The old guards wouldn't use force to prevent the new ones from coming back. They would just discourage the idea. Therefore the proper procedure would be to.

WEARILY, THE guard at the left of the table removed a cud of tobacco from his mouth and heaved it through the open doorway as the new men entered. His companion was stubbornly retrieving two cards which had tucked themselves up his sleeve while he was shuffling the recalcitrant deck. He looked up and smiled in relief at the sight of the replacements. Maybe he would get a little peace now.

Carefully he laid the deck on the table and watched it for a moment. Surprisingly it seemed inclined to accept his authority and remain there.

"Sit down, boys. I'll deal you a hand," he invited, "I'm Edmun and this is Spud."

Spud ejected a flake of tobacco from his mouth and looked triumphant when it plastered itself against the wall. He smiled his welcome.

The newcomers seemed disinclined to join in the game. They announced a desire to look over the prison. It was one they had never been in.

"It's like all the rest of them," Edmun said. "Come on. We need you in the game."

"When I go into a new place," said one of the newcomers, "I like to let the lads in the cells know who I am. So I won't get any nonsense off them later on."

His companion nodded.

"There's only one in there," said Spud. "He won't give any trouble. We don't even have to feed him."

"Don't have to feed him?"

"No. The Duke said to starve him so he'd be more ferocious in the arena tomorrow."

"A prisoner of the Duke's, eh? I'm going to see that boy. The Duke don't often put anybody in jail."

"He's nothing much to look at," Edmun said. "Let's start the game."

The two new guards looked at each other. One spoke the thought which coursed through both their minds: "There's something funny here," he muttered.

"We're going in," the other announced.

"You're wasting your time," said Spud. "Let's play."

The two exchanged glances and came to an unspoken agreement.

"We got lots of time," said one, opening the inner door. The other followed and closed the door. They looked in amazement at Mark and Omega standing among the strange equipment on the corridor floor, and gazed incredulously at the illuminated walls and ceiling.

"Clever," Omega applauded. "Putting that suspicion in their minds did the trick. That's the sort of thing you might have to use tomorrow."

Mark looked speculatively at the guards, who were too astounded to do more than gape. "I'm not so sure that they wouldn't have come back here anyway," he said.

"Try another experiment," Omega suggested. "Something you know very well they won't do. You don't have to be subtle, you know. After all, nobody would believe a guard who accused his prisoner of hypnotizing him. Mow 'em down."

BY THIS time one of the new men got a grip on himself. He drew his sword and stepped forward. He was going to find out very quickly why these prisoners weren't in their cells, and put them where they belonged. And quick.

His eyes bored angrily into Mark's. For some reason his stare didn't seem to have its usual effect. Mark didn't seem to be afraid at all. His eyes were the friendliest the guard had even seen. There couldn't be any harm in a man like that. He stopped, undecided. And then he realized what the whole unusual situation meant.

Dimly he remembered the fellows in the outer room saying something about this fellow participating in the games tomorrow. He had thought that the man was to be one of the victims of the orgy, but he knew now that he had been wrong. This lad was designing some sort of torture machine with which to entertain the crowd in the arena. And the old man was helping him. They were both public-spirited men, anxious to please the throngs who were to witness the holiday games.

He squinted at one of the nearer of the machines. He couldn't make much of it, though the thought occurred to him that if a man was forced to step in it he would certainly get his feet all cut up on those glass tubes and sharp wire ends. A thing like that would be better if it had a knife concealed among those coils.

"Here," he said. "Maybe you can use this."

The sword, with which he had originally intended to force the prisoners back into their cells, he extended to Mark, smiling in his desire to be friendly and helpful.

Mark handed it back, "No," he said, "I don't think I can use it." He picked up the weapons of Edmun and Spud, which were as rigid as they had ever been, and offered these also. "You can return these to the other guards. Now suppose you men go back to the guard room and leave me alone. I want to get this finished before the week is over."

The guards nodded quite happily and went away. They closed the inner door tightly, lest Mark be disturbed by the sound of the card game. They looked sheepishly at the other two guards.

"Why didn't you tell us he was busy and didn't want to be disturbed? Let's start that game."

Edmun and Spud stared at each other uncomprehendingly, as they returned their swords to their belts. They decided not to ask about what had happened inside. Edmun resolutely picked up the deck and dealt four hands, his confidence in his ability to control the cards vastly restored. None of them misbehaved. Spud brightened up, and cut himself a chew of tobacco. For a minute he masticated it furiously and then spat hopefully into a corner. The result was wholly gratifying. He beamed at Edmun and the game went on.

Mark watched the door close and looked at Omega. "If they send soldiers for me tomorrow, it would look funny if those men were out of uniform. Better to let them have their swords."

Omega nodded. "I guess you're satisfied now."

"Perfectly. Handing over their weapons was one thing there was no chance of their doing accidentally. Let's get back to work."

"Go to it," Omega said. "I'm no help to you, so I'll leave you to figure it out for yourself. There are some other things that need my attention. See you later."

The old man's body faded abruptly and was gone. Mark looked at the maze of apparatus spread before him and felt a sudden loneliness. Omega's return had filled him with a new enthusiasm, but with his going it seemed to have gone also. He wished he had never fallen off that cursed boat. It had embroiled him in a set of circumstances which was keeping him from the one place in the world that he wanted to be… at Nona's side.

Yet he knew that he couldn't stop now. He had to finish the job. There would be an eternity of time to enjoy Nona's company, when this work was done. And millions of people would be the happier for his labor. The thought seemed to give him a new vigor. With flying fingers he went back to the intricate wiring.

Heedless of time, he continued to work, while the sun faded in the west and the night began its long, quiet reign. Several times he ripped his wiring apart in exasperation. Once he produced a vibration which seemed to shake the whole building. Cracks appeared in the walls and the cell doors shook and rattled. With a quick glance at his meters he snapped off the current.

The vibration was a very short one, even shorter than the cosmic rays. But it was still far too long to approximate the waves of thought. These seemed to defy his efforts. With a sigh he tried a new hookup. There was an answer to the problem, and he was determined to find it.

CHAPTER XV

THE GALA OF FOOLS

MORNING CAME, THOUGH Mark failed to notice it until he heard the sound of the gongs announcing the end of curfew. Shortly after the sound had throbbed in the silence, Spud appeared, carrying a set of manacles and a leg chain attached to a heavy iron ball.

He stopped short at the sight of the apparatus-littered corridor. The lighted walls he didn't notice, for the sun was streaming in the window.

Mark looked up, disturbed by the rattling of the chains. "Quiet!" he snapped.

Spud looked apologetic. "They'll be coming for you pretty soon," he said. "The people who take part in the games are kept under the stands during the day."

"I really shouldn't spare the time, but I suppose—"

Mark frowned as he held out his hands. Although he had been consistently failing to solve the problem, he had a notion that he might get the answer very soon, just before the ringing of curfew's end, he had experienced a return of the nebulous idea which had popped into his head while Omega had been talking.

But before he could pin it down, curfew had rung and Spud's interruption did the rest.

Somehow he knew that if he could follow the thought through, he would have his answer. It had something to do with the fact that the same machine would produce both the hypnosis wave and the telekinesis wave which would furnish the power for its transmission. The clue lay in the short difference in wave length between the two.

Spud snapped the manacles on his wrists and clamped on an ankle iron. Then he lifted the iron ball and offered it to Mark. Mark took it gravely, and they went into the guard room. Edmun was dozing in a chair; the others weren't in sight. Spud pulled a chair from beneath the table and gave it to Mark. Then he made himself comfortable.

"Tell me about these games," Mark requested, more to pass the time than anything. When the soldiers arrived to escort him to the arena, they would have no reason for going back into the prison for their man. And from Spud's viewpoint, it would be much better for no one to know that Mark had pretty much the run of the prison. And it was equally desirable, for Mark, that no outsider learn of any unusual doings here.

Spud's eyes lit up at the thought of the games. Suddenly voluble, he recounted the things he had seen during the celebrations of previous harvest festivals. As he talked, Mark felt a chill taking form inside him, gripping frostily at the pit of a long disused stomach. Spud wasn't describing a series of games at all.

The Duke had said that he thought Mark would have an even chance of surviving a week of these events, and Mark had visualized some sort of primitive rough and tumble where men's limbs were in danger. Some form of game in which sides would be formed and men would pit their strength and durability against one another. Hazardous and brutal, but not necessarily fatal.

But Spud was gleefully and with elaborate detail describing a simple routine for slaughter. He told of unarmed men pitted in mortal combat against equal numbers of armed and armored soldiers; of fights between prisoners armed with daggers; of animals from lands far to the south stalking men and women trapped within the arena.

Mark shuddered. And these barbarians were the people he was trying to help. For a long minute he contemplated giving up the whole idea of the rebellion. If this was the sort of thing that they liked, they weren't worth lifting a hand for.

BUT THEN he remembered a certain news picture he had seen when an apparently high state of civilization had flourished on the earth. It had dealt with a public hanging which had taken place in his own country. The picture had shown a morbid throng standing on tiptoe, that no gruesome detail would be missed. A mother was holding aloft a small girl.

And only a short step further back in the history of his people there had existed barbarities of almost the same sort as the ones that Spud was so gleefully describing. Accused witches had been burned at the stake. Small boys had been put to death in this very land for the heinous offense of throwing stones at the constabulary. Torture was an established institution in the good

Christian days of Richard, the Lion-Hearted—and even later. Scientists of a few hundred years prior to Mark's birth had been stoned and burned for the crime of consorting with Satan.

Yet the close descendants of the very people who had fostered all this, were the humane and kindly, the enlightened peoples of the twentieth century. Had human character changed so abruptly in the course of a few hundred years? Hardly.

If conditions were changed so that the Brish could consider themselves free human beings, the more humane aspects of their natures would come out. He hoped.

Mark knew that he still felt surges of primitive savagery within him. Such instincts, of course, only came to the fore during the heat of battle, but they were there, nevertheless. And he was the product of a gentler era. It was natural that during the present age of misery and suppression, the tougher elements of human nature should predominate. But the very fact that the gentle Jon, Duke of Scarbor, was a man of some popularity, proved that the better instincts still survived.

Having settled this point in his mind, Mark became even more determined to go on with his plans.

"Get those two new guardsmen in here," he commanded. Spud, interrupted in his glowing story of the games, stared, then jumped to obey. He returned in a minute with the others, who were red-eyed and angry at being disturbed.

"Waken Edmun," Mark directed. "And all four of you sit side by side on that bench."

Wonderingly, the guards obeyed. Mark faced them with a stare. In a few moments their eyes glazed, the lids drooped wearily.

"On the floor at your feet," he said, "you see pieces of sandstone. The blades of your daggers could use a little sharpening."

All four drew their weapons and glanced stupidly at the gleaming blades. Then, as one man, they reached down as if for the piece of sandstone. There followed a brilliant performance of the motions used to sharpen knife-blades. Mark was satisfied that the men were fully under his control.

"That's enough," he said. "Replace your knives and drop the sandstone. Now, listen carefully. In the prison corridor are several machines which are extremely dangerous to touch. Don't for any reason go near them. If any new prisoners are brought in, take them to the cell block on the top floor. Sudden death awaits the man who molests those machines!"

Nodding his satisfaction, Mark woke the guards. That ought to do the trick.

IT WAS perhaps a half-hour later when a peremptory hammering sounded on the outer door. Spud answered it, and in strode a soldier who had been with Jon when Mark had been snatched from Erlayok's torture chamber, accompanied by another, who had helped Erlayok in the same chamber. A sudden suspicion flashed in Mark's mind. He remembered the cat-ate-the-canary expression that he had last seen on Erlayok's face. A possible explanation seemed to suggest itself in the presence of this man.

"Why are you here?" he demanded.

Erlayok's man grinned maliciously. "To see that you get what's coming to you," he informed. "Erlayok runs the show, you know. And he'd be disappointed if his star performer didn't show up. He doesn't trust the likes of this lad here."

Jon's man paid no attention. Mark guessed that this wasn't the first insult he had swallowed on the way over. But he had evidently been given strict orders from the Duke to stay out of any battles which might interfere with his job.

"And you're here," Mark guessed, "to see that I do my performing in the arena only, and not to an audience of Erlayok's men?"

"Exactly," the man said, smiling. "I'm Chumly. The Duke's orders were to see that you are protected. But of course you'll be on your own when you enter the arena. Shall we start?"

Erlayok's man made an insolent gesture and mimicked, "Shall we start?" Then he roared with laughter. Mark reflected sadly that Erlayok's men all seemed to own a lamentable sense of humor. He turned to Chumly. "A real wit, your friend."

"On the way over I decided he resembled some obnoxious little dog, yapping at his betters," Chumly replied. "But on the other hand, a dog has some admirable characteristics, even those little yappers. On second thought I should say he reminds me of some dirty, wallowing pig. I've noticed something of the odor, too. He needs a bath."

With a roar of rage Erlayok's man, whipped out his sword and started for Chumly. Mark stopped him with a look. The weapon clattered to the flagstones of the courtyard, and a glassiness replaced the anger in the man's eyes.

"You're a hybrid," Mark stated. "The spawn of a dog and a sow."

The man promptly dropped to all fours and waddled across the court behind them, yapping occasionally in a dejected sort of way.

Chumly looked back at him and chuckled. "That's a trick worth knowing," he said. "His Highness told me you were an unusual man, but I didn't expect anything like this. You stand a good chance of coming out of that arena alive." He said the last in a voice which implied that such things were practically unheard of.

Mark scarcely heard him. So Jon had said that he was an unusual man. Mark tried to think why. His action in stopping the runaways could have been done as well by a thousand other men. It might have been that business of bending the cell bars, but Mark didn't think so. Then he remembered the Duke's dramatic entrance in to the torture chamber. Had the Duke seen his flesh emerge unblemished from the branding iron? But he had made no mention of it. And certainly his surprise would have been equal to that of Erlayok and his men. He would surely have questioned Mark once they were out of the place. Unless he already knew....

"When you rescued me yesterday, did you break right in,

or were you outside that room for a while before the Duke entered?"

"We were there for a few minutes," Chumly answered. "The Duke stood outside the door and looked in. The rest of us couldn't see anything, but I could bear the Earl talking. The Duke broke in when they were going to burn out one of your eyes." Chumly's admiration for his companion showed in his face. "You sure held out on them, didn't you?"

That answered the question in Mark's mind. The Duke *did* know. He became more convinced when he considered the fact that only two guards were being used to escort him to the arena. Erlayok had sent his man merely to check up on Jon, to be sure that he didn't let Mark escape. But Erlayok probably thought that Jon would dispatch several soldiers for the errand. And the fact that only one of the Duke's men was sent to guard him, meant that the Duke might want to give Mark an opportunity to escape. Or it might also mean that Jon knew that Mark had no intention of escaping. His attempt to puzzle out the possibilities of the situation was interrupted by a commotion to the rear.

The antics of Erlayok's man were attracting due attention. He was doing his very best to carry out Mark's command by behaving in the probable style of the hybrid he firmly believed he was. He barked and then grunted, alternately.

Upon their arrival, Mark broke the spell, but not until several of the soldiers present had seen him bury his face into a pile of garbage, barking happily as he did so. Chumly removed Mark's chains, and joined the other soldiers.

THE ARENA was like a huge ball-park. The stands would easily hold the population of a fair-sized city. The prisoners were herded into spaces beneath them. Dozens of soldiers were guarding the doorway which led to the street, but only one was stationed at the barred portal entering the arena pit.

Mark's nose was assailed by a multitude of odors, all offensive. The predominant one was of close-packed humanity, and that was the least pleasant of all. Mingled with it was a variety of others originating from other such enclosures as the one he was in. These were animal odors, and among them he detected the strong fragrance of the lion. This was probably one of Spud's "animals from lands far to the south."

From his position near the barred door to the arena he could see that the stands were rapidly filling up. Evidently the entertainment was to last for the better part of the day, for he noticed that many of the spectators were carrying packages of food. Directly opposite the prisoners' pen was a series of ornate boxes, equipped with plush seats, and attended by uniformed lackeys. Obviously these were reserved for the nobles and their families. Some of them were already occupied by gaudily dressed men and jewel bedecked women.

THERE WAS a sudden murmur in the stands when one of the boxes, a prominently situated one, was almost filled by the gross bulk of Erlayok. Behind him came two young women, richly appareled, who seated themselves at his side. Handsome and assured, they were quite apparently members of mankind's oldest and most enduring profession.

Erlayok looked about him. He frowned as he noted that the most elaborate of all the boxes was still empty. This one was no doubt the one reserved for Jon. And the Earl was probably piqued that he should have to wait for the appearance of one whom he considered a useless puppet.

Mark grinned, and hoped that Jon would keep him waiting for an hour. He was disappointed, though, for scarcely had Erlayok made himself comfortable when the Duke appeared, alone. The murmur which arose as the crowd saw him, deepened Erlayok's frown. Jon was obviously the more popular man.

The first event was one which was calculated to start the day off with a bang. A stentorian-voiced announcer described it to the avid spectators. Four condemned men were to be forced into the pit, each armed with a dagger. A lion would then be loosed. The cheer which greeted the announcement told Mark that this was evidently the sort of spectacle the people wanted. He experienced a momentary return of the revulsion he had felt before.

The feeling left when he noticed the expression of distaste on Jon's face. The Duke sat alone, and this further cheered Mark. It indicated that although Jon was obliged to attend this affair, due to his position, his family didn't care to.

He was suddenly jolted by a rough shove from behind. Wheeling, he saw the face of the man he had humbled in the street. He was leering in a most horrible manner.

"It's your turn now," he grated, handing Mark a short dagger and brandishing a borrowed sword to protect himself. "Let's see you go out there and stick that in the lion." He burst into gales of laughter at the thought of anybody managing to do any harm to a lion with such a puny weapon. Mark took a deep breath and went....

CHAPTER XVI

THE HAPPY WARRIOR

SOLDIERS STOOD BEHIND the three other victims, ready to force them into the arena. But it wasn't necessary. The iron door swung open and the four stepped out. Mark looked around to see where the lion was coming from, but it was impossible to tell. There were doors on all sides of the enclosure and the lion might be dispatched through any one of them.

The other three evidently reasoned the same way, for they immediately went toward the center of the pit. That point was the farthest away from all the doors.

Mark followed slowly, tossing his dagger aloft and catching it dexterously by the handle. He didn't feel nearly as sure of himself as he looked, but at least he was making a nice impression.

He reached the place in the middle of the pit where the other three were standing, and went on toward Erlayok's box.

He guessed that the lion wouldn't be loosed immediately. The crowd would be first given a display of the breaking nerves of the victims, waiting, for a rending, slashing death to claim them. Mark was spoiling the show, if that was what they were expecting.

His nonchalant tossing and catching of the dagger not only attracted every eye in the stands, but served to somewhat calm the nerves of the other three. They watched him too, though they were also watching out for the entrance of the lion.

"Erlayok," called Mark, loud enough for a good portion of the stands to hear. "After I kill this lion, will you meet me down here in a man-to-man combat? My dagger against whatever weapons you wish?"

Erlayok's face worked as he listened to the yells of the spectators. The majority, it seemed, were delighted with the proposal. Mark tried to maintain a noncommittal appearance, but some of them had gleams in their eyes which might have meant that they also approved.

Jon openly clapped his hands. Erlayok's eyes darted from side to side, as if trying to memorize the faces of as many as possible of those who would like to see him in the pit.

"Loose the lion!" he roared suddenly.

MARK LAUGHED and turned back toward the other men. The lion came and as Mark had earlier suspected, it came from one of the doors quite close to the one from which he and the other had emerged. The odor had been too strong for the lion cages to be at any great distance.

The arrangement had apparently been made so that the slaughter would take place very close to the nobles' seats. The commoners were way out by left field, so to speak, with the sun in their eyes.

Three of the victims ran with all their might directly away from the big cat, and their flight took them right toward the boxes of the nobles. But the fourth didn't.

Casually Mark strode toward the door from which the lion

Mark leaped on the lion's back, raised
his dagger, and prayed

emerged. For a moment the beast seemed to be bewildered, not sure what to do with his newfound freedom. His nostrils flared as he sniffed the air, turning his head to take in the whole arena. Then he froze, sighting Mark. Mark was by far the biggest and most appetizing of the four, and that lion knew good flesh from skin and bones when he saw it.

Mark tensed. In spite of his peculiar endowment, he was a man, and man instinctively feels a surge of fear when facing the king of beasts. And this one was a peculiarly savage and unpleasant specimen. He was obviously hungry, and his hide quivered over quite visible ribs.

Leo crouched, his tail twitching. He opened his fanged mouth to give the roar which would strike terror to the heart of this brash human. At that moment Mark snapped out of it. This, he figured, was the moment when his opponent should spring, and it was during this moment when he must make the move which would win the battle.

And his guess was right.

As the soul-chilling roar rent the air, the bunched muscles of the crouching beast extended themselves in the leap which should have brought the puny man beneath the outstretched claws. In that split second Mark leaped forward also and swerved just out of the path of those slashing talons. Like the broken-field runner he once was, he wheeled suddenly as the lion passed him.

A prodigious leap carried him astride the lion's back, the fingers of one hand buried in his mane. His knees dug into the beast's sides and he clung like a leech.

Startled, the lion reared. He received a series of annoying stabs through the shoulder muscles for his pains. Then he tried rolling on his back. This move almost broke Mark's ribs, but he hung on.

"Whoa, Bessie!" Mark howled. He was stabbing repeatedly in a number of places within the reach of his hand, trying to find the beast's heart. But either he was missing the spot, or the dagger was too short, for the animal continued his frantic efforts to throw him off.

Then suddenly the lion succeeded! After rolling over for the third time, he came to his feet and gave a convulsive leap. It was a move Mark had failed to anticipate. The beast's back bowed and then abruptly arched, tearing the clinging man's knee-hold loose.

Mark landed sitting, the dagger torn from his hand. He was on his feet instantly, facing the lion.

He could see the hilt of the knife, almost invisible in the folds of flesh beneath the animal's shoulder. If he could duplicate his former acrobatic feat when the beast leaped again, he would be able to retrieve it and continue stabbing.

Then suddenly he realized it wasn't necessary. The lion didn't crouch for another leap. It weaved unsteadily for a moment, then collapsed, dead! The little knife had found its mark!

Mark reached over and drew it out of the carcass, wiping it on the animal's mane.

A TUMULT arose from the stands. People were standing on their seat and cheering wildly. Mark bowed and then started for Erlayok's box. The stadium quieted as he approached.

"Are you going to accept that challenge?" Mark called. "Your sword is surely equal to my dagger. Lower your fat behind down off that perch, and let your people see how brave you are."

Another clamor arose. By this time the Earl had recovered his poise. He smiled as if amused at the offer.

"You wish to give the crowd some more entertainment, of course," he said. "It would be another crime to add to your record if you are making this challenge only for the purpose of doing harm to a noble of the Land of the Brish. Therefore I assume that you really have a better motive in mind. You wish to entertain the populace gathered here. Am I right?"

Mark saw what was coming, but there was nothing he could do about it. If he answered any way but the affirmative, there would be another crime to add to him. And that would mean that instead of going free at the end of these games, he would have to stand trial once more. And that might seriously interfere with his plans.

"I wish only to entertain these good people," he said. "But I am sure that can be best accomplished in the way I suggest. You have boasted of being able to handle me by yourself. Come down and prove it!"

"It *has* been proved," claimed Erlayok. "I handled you once before. But there is another way you can do service to the citizens assembled here." He paused and looked about him, benignly. A murmur arose, but Mark couldn't tell what it meant. Erlayok continued: "You will be given the axe which was taken from you when you were imprisoned. With it you may demonstrate your skill against five of my best warriors!"

There was no doubt of the meaning of the shouts which followed. The spectators wanted more blood. It didn't matter to them that Mark had entertained them well already. They were perfectly willing to see him slaughtered as long as the sport was worth watching. Mark thought back to the vagaries of the prize-fight crowds he had seen in years when there had been prize-fights. Human nature hadn't changed much. A mob was still a mob. The lowest form of disorganized humanity.

The shriek of a siren suddenly cut through the noise of the crowd's cheering. Mark saw that the sound came from a hand-operated contrivance in the announcer's box. He was pointing toward the loge of Jon, Duke of Scarbor. The Duke was stand-ing, waiting for silence.

"People of Scarbor!" he began. "You are not living up to the principles of good sportsmanship for which our citizens are renowned. This man has earned the right to rest until tomor-row's games. The rules of the contests are so written."

The Duke sat down amidst a murmur of disappointment. But Erlayok rose and waved his hands. When the crowd again became silent he bowed in the direction of the Duke and smiled a sardonic smile.

"We must not forget that this man volunteered to entertain once more today," he reminded, turning toward Mark. "Is that not your desire?"

Mark noticed a certain anxiety appear on the face of Jon. That made him feel a lot better. He bowed deeply toward the ornate loge. He saw an opportunity of turning the capricious favor of the crowd. A favor which appeared for the moment to be directed toward Erlayok.

"I shall fight," he announced, "for I know that the good Duke wishes to see his subjects amused. Only his high sense of justice moves him to give me a chance to reconsider. Long live the Duke!"

THE TUMULT which followed made all former cheering sound feeble. Among those present in the arena were people from all parts of the duchy. And Mark wanted Jon's popular-ity to be increased. For the popularity of the Duke in no way interfered with the coming rebellion. The majority of the people already knew of the Duke's efforts to alleviate oppression, and they had no antagonism for him.

Their hatred was centered on the nobles who nullified those efforts. It was important, however, that these contests not reflect any advantage to the nobles. And taking the credit for this coming battle away from Erlayok was a step in the right direction.

In a few minutes the carcass of the king of beasts had been dragged away, and fresh sand sprinkled over the spot where his blood had made the ground slippery. The three men whose lives had been spared by Mark's victory were herded back into the prisoners' quarters under the stands. They were afforded a reprieve until tomorrow's games would again place their lives in jeopardy.

A door opened beneath the box where Erlayok and his women sat. Out marched five of the most formidable men Mark had seen since coming to the Land of the Brish. Or ever.

Two of them were about Mark's size. The other three were bigger and much heavier. Their thickset bodies were protected by the steel breastplates which were standard equipment of the soldiers of this land. And each carried a dirk in the left hand, in addition to a broad battle-axe. Mark's own axe and dagger looked puny and ineffectual by comparison.

As they came toward him it was apparent that they had hastily formulated a plan of action before entering the arena. They spread out crescent-like, obviously intent upon circling him. Confidence was mirrored on their faces. One of them even looked embarrassed.

Mark had never seen these men before, but no doubt they had been told of his ability. He foresaw their clumsy attempt to surround him, and leaped instantly into action. The warrior on the far left was one of the larger three. As Mark sprang toward him he snarled and aimed his ponderous weapon in a sweeping slash at Mark's neck. Mark checked his rush just enough to let it whistle past.

For the instant the warrior was completely helpless as the momentum of his swing turned him halfway around. That instant was his last. Mark's flashing axe caught him in exactly the spot he had intended to strike Mark. His severed jugular pumped a crimson, gushing stream.

The speed with which it was done made the spectators gasp. Sudden cheers went up. All sorts of advice was shouted, most of it inexpert and all of it quite useless. They might as well have been shouting: "Moider dat bum!"

But it was not as simple as all that. These warriors were not tyros. When the first man had gone down, they knew immediately that there was a serious business ahead of them. And they took no foolish chances.

Their adversary had shown a speed that no single one of them could match. They gave up their tactics of spreading out and trying to encircle him. That system gave his superior speed a chance to pick them off one by one. Instead they closed up and attacked him in a body. The two center men engaged him in a furious attack while the two outer ones kept pecking at him and trying to get far enough to the sides to deliver blows he could not ward off.

Back across the arena the battle waged, Mark giving ground to prevent the maneuver from being completed. He made sudden leaps to the side from time to time in an effort to get a second or two in which he would be facing only one man.

But each time he tried this, the man he had singled out for individual attack moved back to join the others. Mark was continually facing the massed front of the four.

THE FIERCE tempo of the battle kept the audience in an uproar. But even above the shouts of the crowd, the ringing impact of axe on axe could be heard with the regularity of a triphammer.

An occasional rasping, spine chilling shriek rent the air as a parried axe slid across the blade of a dagger. This was always followed by a clanging thud, for the sound only came when one of the warriors expertly used his dirk to deflect Mark's axe so that it struck futilely against his breastplate.

Mark's dagger was almost useless, being several inches shorter than those of Erlayok's men, and too light to use for such a purpose.

Once a roar arose which drowned out all other sound as Mark countered an axe-swing which he had managed to duck, and used his dirk in a backhand stab. The soldier who received it suddenly sprang back from the mêlée, clutching a thigh. But he was back again in a minute.

Mark had felt his dirk sheath itself in the man's leg. Out of the corner of his eye he had seen the man retire. But the remaining three, also seeing the odds go down, pressed him with renewed vigor. For a few minutes he was so busy dodging and countering that he was forced to keep every sense alert to avoid the three. When the injured men returned to the battle he came from the rear, and Mark had no warning of his coming.

Fortunately for him the snarling soldier on his right aimed a terrific axe-blow at his head at that precise moment. And the man in front lunged forward, aiming for his middle. Mark smacked aside the head-blow with his own axe, and was forced to leap to the left and backward to avoid being disemboweled by the other man. At that instant a battle-axe flashed downward through the spot he had just vacated. The blow would have split him from crown to groin.

From that instant the tide of battle changed. The descending axe buried itself in the ground at Mark's side. Mark's left hand was brushed by the hair of the man who had wielded it. The man had been carried forward and down by the force of the blow. Mark was only half aware that the sable wings of death had almost enfolded him.

He was too busy with the men facing him to permit his attention to waver for an instant. But nevertheless the contact of that hair with his hand caused a reflex in Mark's perfectly trained body. His hand twisted and the dirk drove a slanting course from a point beneath the right ear, burying itself to the hilt. The man slumped, lifeless.

Mark left the dagger where it was. He had no further use for it.

Now the odds were really three to one. And for Mark that meant virtually an even battle. If anything, slightly in his favor. It was almost certain that he could prevent them from inflicting any telling damage. With the four he had been in constant danger that one of them would maneuver far enough to the side to deliver a blow he couldn't block. Several such blows, in fact, had already landed. And though they had all been flesh wounds, instantly healed, there had been the ever present possibility that one of them would cleave his brain and do damage that couldn't be repaired.

But now that risk was gone. No three men lived who could move fast enough to get around him. And the battle was speedily going in his favor for an entirely different reason.

These warriors were powerful men and well trained, but they were, after all, only men, and subject to natural exhaustion.

And the longer they wielded their heavy axes, the more they tired. Gone was their strategy and coördination. They no longer seemed to have any plan of battle. Each man was concentrating on his own survival and vainly hoping one of the others would manage to bring down this dancing demon.

Mark, by contrast, was as fresh and flashy as yellow daisies in a meadow. For he was tapping the energy waves given off from the slowly disintegrating radioactive element in his blood. It was a source of power which provided more energy than he could possibly use by physical exercise. He was eternally fresh and untiring, while his opponents showed their fatigue in their twisted faces and in their gulping gasps for air.

ABRUPTLY MARK leaped backward several steps. Dazed, the panting three plodded after. Their eyes were fixed dully, hopelessly upon him. They knew they were doomed but kept coming, determined to fight as long as they could move. Mark kept backing away, keeping them at a safe distance.

"Erlayok's got you into this," he told them, talking rapidly. "He knew what would happen. Why not get back at him while there is still a chance?" Their dazed eyes told him nothing. He continued, speaking only loud enough for them to hear. "I'm taking you toward his box. When you get close enough, throw your axes at him. You're going to die anyway. Do something useful while you're about it. He had no mercy on you, knowing that you were certain to be defeated."

But the idea backfired. If Mark had hypnotized them, they would have obeyed his suggestion. But they were fighting men, following the orders of their master, and he wouldn't take that advantage. Otherwise he could have ended the contest long ago.

As it was his suggestion about throwing their axes gave one of them an idea. Mark suddenly found himself dodging the flying weapon of the largest of the three remaining warriors. It had been accurately thrown, but lightning reflexes came to his rescue.

It passed safely over his head.

Still retreating, Mark scooped it up and heaved it back. He aimed it low and it landed where he intended. The blade cut deep into the man's leg, below the knee, and down he went—permanently out of the battle.

Neither of the remaining two was willing to chance the loss of his weapon. They continued to press forward. Mark, with a burst of speed, dashed toward them and to the left. They turned to face him, sluggishly. The maneuver placed one behind the other. The man in front raised his axe to deliver a blow. But the blow never landed.

With a movement so fast that it appeared that his arm blurred for an instant, he brought the flat of his axe down on the man's biceps. The cumbersome battle-axe thudded to the ground, the arm which had wielded it, broken.

The last man stared stupidly, too far gone to offer any resistance. His axe dangled loosely in his hand. Mark, suddenly pitying him, stepped forward and let him have his left fist on the point of the jaw. The man dropped like an ox.

The crowd cheered wildly.

Mark sensed that it approved his actions in sparing the lives of the last three men. The spectators were bloodthirsty, but these three had put up a fine battle, and deserved better than death. The thought that man retained some mercy in his makeup pleased Mark immensely. His actions, however, wouldn't have been changed even if the mob had been crying for the blood of these three.

CHAPTER XVII

NIGHT PROMENADE

MARK WATCHED THE rest of the day's bloody program from the prisoners' quarters beneath the stands. After a while he became inured to the barbarities he saw. They ceased to make his blood boil as they had at first. It was like the pity one might feel when witnessing for the first time a scene in an abattoir. After a certain number of repetitions, the thing seems to be devoid of any reality in the way of pain or suffering. There is also the realization that such things must be and that there was nothing could be done about it.

But there was a difference. For although Mark realized that there was nothing he could do at the present time, nor for years to come, he also knew that if his plans were successful, there would certainly be a lesser demand for such exhibitions in the future.

Eventually the last contest was finished and a weary, sated crowd made for the exits. For the moment they'd reached their limit, but they would be back in the morning, keener than ever.

Mark dived into his work that night with a new determination.

His zeal, however, seemed to have no bearing on his work. The solution of the problem eluded him as it had the night before. When morning came and the first rays of the sun told him that he would shortly have to return to the arena, he was as far from success as he had been when he started. Further, in one way. When he had begun this work there had been several ideas in his mind, several methods he could use to attack the problem. Since then he had tried them all, and failed consistently.

The second day at the arena passed drearily. He didn't make the mistake of letting himself in for a double performance. One was enough. It left him as near nauseated as it was possible for him to be.

A dozen of the most hardened criminals and he among them, were chosen for a battle royale. The announcer was particular to state that it was a battle to the death. Mark suspected that this was a device of Erlayok's to insure that every man involved would do his best to do away with Erlayok's pet hate, Mark. The battle was conducted without any but nature's weapons, and the fact gave Mark a chance to thwart the Earl's designs. He went to work furiously, knocking men unconscious, and occasionally breaking arms. One particularly tough specimen gave so much trouble that he was obliged to break a leg.

So thoroughly and swiftly did he work at the business of putting men out of the battle without actually killing them, that only one of the other eleven was killed. The killer later received the one broken leg in the event. And the crowd was just as pleased as if gore had run by the bucketful.

Mark saw Erlayok's frown and grinned as he left the arena. He gave the grin for the sole purpose of infuriating the Earl, who was looking at him. He wanted Erlayok to know that he had been outwitted.

INSIDE, HE didn't feel at all like grinning. His performance had left a bad taste in his mouth. Knocking men cold didn't bother him. They fell without a sound. But those who had grappled with him and forced him to wrestle and finally break bones, had spoiled his equanimity.

It is seldom that a bone is broken without being accompanied by an involuntary scream of pain. Those screams, and the moaning and groaning which followed got under his skin. Today, as never before, Mark conceived an active distaste for dealing out physical punishment. Never before had he gone about such a task in cold blood as he had today.

That evening, as the throbbing of the curfew faded and died, he again threw his energy into the seemingly endless task of duplicating the hypnosis wave. His only progress had been negative. He had proved that none of his ideas were feasible. Every one had resulted in failure. Several times he had produced vibrations which had almost shaken the prison down on him, but they were useless, and taught him nothing. The extremely short wave which he needed seemed impossible to produce mechanically.

And on this night he seemed to be getting no nearer a solution. He tried several variations of the ideas he had worked on previously and accomplished nothing of value. Finally in disgust he tossed a wrench he had been using directly into the middle of the latest hookup he had contrived. There was a short series of popping sounds as a bank of delicate vacuum tubes upset and exploded.

He gazed morosely at the wreckage, heedless of the damage he had done. "All right," he muttered. "Blow up. Collapse. Phooey!"

Abruptly he strode to the door into the guardroom and shoved it open. Edmun and Spud were dozing in their chairs, but awoke and jumped to their feet. The others weren't in sight.

"You two would be better off in bed," Mark growled. I sound, he thought, just like Aunt Nellie. Working too hard. Getting no place. Nuts.

"We've got to guard you," Spud explained. "So you don't escape."

Mark snorted. "Don't be silly."

Spud grinned cheerfully. "Sure. You'd just bend a few bars and walk out."

"Exactly," Mark answered. "So you might as well go to bed. *I'm* going out for a walk. I'll be back before morning. Don't lock the door after me."

The guards looked stupidly at each other as Mark drew the iron bolts of the outer door. As he went out and closed the door they shrugged and resumed their interrupted naps.

MARK WALKED briskly. He had no particular destination. He had decided on the walk because he thought the cool night air might set his brain to working more clearly. He breathed great volumes of the stuff into his lungs, with no apparent effect. His brain didn't suddenly jump to the solution of his problem. If anything, his thoughts became the more chaotic. His mind kept leaping back to one after another of the experiments which had failed, trying to put a mental finger on the reason for the failure.

He was getting angry with himself. He shouldn't be fruitlessly rehashing his former ideas. He had proved they wouldn't work. But there seemed no other line of thought to pursue. The devices he had tried encompassed practically all that was known in his time concerning ultra-short waves. And yet some other attack to the problem was obviously indicated. But in what direction would he make the attack?

Abruptly he stopped taking the deep breaths. It had come to him why they weren't doing anything toward clearing his foggy brain. Deep breaths did nothing but oxygenate the blood. And since his blood had no particular use for oxygen, he was accomplishing nothing. There wasn't anything wrong with his brain anyway. It was working all right. The trouble was that he had allowed it to become enmeshed in a maze of circuitous thought. He would have to forget the whole problem. And when he came back to it later he might be able to tackle the thing from a new angle.

A flurry of motion in the block ahead of him brought him to

an abrupt stop. Peering intently toward the spot, he discerned the forms of several men. The night watch!

He wheeled and retraced his steps, swiftly and silently. At the next corner he turned to the left and continued his rapid walking. The incident served to make him even angrier. For a second he contemplated turning back and doing battle with them. He was just in the proper mood to vent his feelings by cracking a few skulls. But he thought better of it when he considered the remote possibility that he wouldn't be able to cope successfully with a score of armed men, weaponless himself.

A few minutes after the turn-off he began to recognize where he was. A short distance from Smid's haberdashery, the rebel headquarters. He decided that as long as he was this close he would stop and say hello to Murf.

Above Smid's door was a small number plate, identical in appearance with a dozen others in the street. It had a peculiarity of its own, however. Members of a close circle of rebel leaders knew that it was attached to a cord which would ring a bell if the numberplate were pulled out from the wall. And if, the proper number of pulls were made, at the proper intervals, Smid would open the door at any time of the day or night.

Mark gave the signal.

Smid peered through a peephole and then opened the door, his eyes wide with surprise. Mark slipped inside.

"Praise to the gods!" Smid exclaimed. "You managed to escape!"

Smid's welcome made Mark feel fine, and once more he understood that there were human beings after all among these savages.

Smid hurriedly led the way to the cellar where he awakened Murf, who was snoring gently on a cot. Murf opened one eye, saw Mark, then jumped to his feet. Delightedly he pumped Mark's hand. "I thought you'd never come," he said. "Any hue and cry?"

Mark smiled. "No, and there won't be any. I'm going back before morning."

CHAPTER XVIII

HIS MASTER'S VOICE

SMID'S JAW DROPPED and Murf began to sputter. Mark saw that he would have to explain. This he did, omitting to mention the incredible Omega. Nor did he tell anything about his own past, but explained his knowledge of the forces he was trying to control by saying that such things were known to the wise men of his own land. His confederates took him to mean Norway, and he didn't set them right. The explanation of the hypnosis wave was enough for uninitiated minds to absorb at one sitting. As they sat on the opposite side of a table, listening attentively, he marveled that they could accept even that much without challenging his veracity.

As he talked he saw that Smid's eyes gleamed with a patriotic fervor when he told of how the wave could be directed to enclose the Land of the Brish so that no enemy could attack. The man was envisioning his people freed of the burden of the parasitic armies which had bled them white for so long. His face was ecstatic at the thought.

Murf seemed not nearly so enthusiastic. He frowned when Mark said that the rebellion would best be delayed until he had finished his machines. Time would be needed to place the machines in strategic positions so that the many enemies of the Brish would be kept at bay while the rebels went about their task of ousting the nobles from authority.

Murf nodded unconsciously when Mark pointed out the fact that during the course of the rebellion the frontiers would be left inadequately guarded. Some of the nobles were certain to escape and muster their soldiers in an attempt to retake their strongholds. But when Mark went on to explain that the rebellion was less apt to blow up in their faces if the border was protected by the machines, Murf objected.

"I can't see it," he claimed. "If we place your machines in operation there will be no need for the nobles' forces to stay at the borders. And if they are brought back to the cities, our rebellion is hopeless. We'd be outnumbered ten to one."

Mark shook his head. "But we won't wait a minute after the machines are working," he said. "We'll attack immediately. The armies won't leave the borders, at least not many of them, because they won't know they aren't needed there."

"That's only guesswork," Murf said. "Spies and scouts are going back and forth across the borders all the time. From what you've told me, your machine will keep people from crossing the borders from either direction. The Brish will discover the barrier as quickly as the Mics."

Mark's eyes narrowed. Something in the way Murf had said that started him thinking along lines which weren't at all pleasant.

Why did he speak of the Brish in the third person? Mark remembered that Murf had done this before. Smid always said "we," or "our men." And why had Murf immediately spoken of the Mics? There was another border, on the north, and hundreds of miles of coastline involved.

Mark frowned. He didn't want to complete his uneasy thoughts. He liked Murf and couldn't forget that on more than one occasion the man had done him services and risked his life doing them.

SMID DECIDED to voice an opinion. "I think that nothing of the sort will happen," he said. "Anyone approaching the barrier will be stricken with an overpowering sensation of fear. He won't be able to go on. Now do you think that a spy or scout will go back to his superiors and admit that he suddenly got a touch of cowardice? Most soldiers would desert before they would do that. Therefore, the only chance that the barrier will be discovered would be for a large body of men to try to cross it together. And that won't happen from our side of the lines. Our armies are purely defensive. We're too well hemmed in to launch an attack at any one point."

Mark grinned, forgetting his former thoughts. "That's an idea I hadn't considered," he told Smid. "I guess that just about clinches the argument. What about it, Murf?"

"It's a good point," Murf conceded. "When will the machines be completed?"

"I've been stuck for the last few days," Mark confessed. "But I hope to solve the problem before the end of the week."

"And how long will it take to construct enough of them to take care of the worst of the borders?"

"Another week at the most."

Murf looked at Smid triumphantly. "Can't be done," he said. "Our men are ready to start on a moment's notice, right now! All over the duchy our recruits have been instructed to keep themselves available for instant action. Right in this building are housed the dispatch riders who will round them up when I give the word. Three of them will notify our groups in the other duchies.

"Every man has his instructions where to get his arms and where to go from there. The whole thing has been timed and calculated to the second! Farmers, artisans and laborers' from every corner of the country will proceed singly to the strategic points of attack we agreed upon. When they come together it will be a complete surprise to the nobles. We shall win!

"But we can't wait much longer. These mobilization orders were issued when you told me that you would escape as soon as possible. That was three days ago. Men can't be kept keyed up, waiting to risk their lives, forever. The attack must come very soon. Be reasonable!

"We have planned so well that it isn't likely the nobles will be able to get any word to the border armies. And if some of them do, they will leave enough of a force to slow up any attempted invasion. And what's the difference if there is a little fighting at the border? It would keep the army too busy to bother us."

For a long minute there was a heavy silence. Mark noticed that Smid seemed to have responded to Murf's logic. But the idea of fighting at the border didn't appeal to Mark.

He foresaw that if some of the border soldiers were recalled by the nobles, the remainder, knowing that rebellion was under way in the interior wouldn't be able to put up very good resistance. Soldiers like to know that there is unity and accord in the higher command which sends them to battle. Once those remaining soldiers got the idea that they might be forsaken by their own people; that reïnforcements might fail to relieve them; and that food and other supplies might not be forthcoming when needed, they would be very apt to cut and run.

"You're right—in one respect," Mark said. "Men can't be kept keyed up indefinitely. So suppose you send your patch riders out the first thing in the morning. Have them pass the word for our men to relax and return to their normal occupations. But to keep themselves handy so that they may be given new orders in about two weeks. At that time we will give them two or three days' notice of the day of attack. Things will operate just as smoothly then as they would now. The delay will cause no harm to our plans, and there will be much less bloodshed."

"Two weeks!" Murf burst out. "Don't you realize that the holidays will be over then? We've planned on the present confusion helping us, making it hard for the nobles to round up their forces in time to stop us."

"That's a minor point when you think it over," Mark said. "We're going to strike the strongholds of all nobles at the same time. So confusion or no confusion, they won't be able to get help in time to stop us. When that help does come, we'll be in control."

Murf bit his lip and nodded. They had been figuring on the confusion helping them, but it wasn't such a great necessity. He couldn't very well claim that it was. It appeared that he had lost the argument. Mark would have his delay and the borders would be protected before the attack was made.

Mark saw that he had won, and at the same time he saw something else.

ACROSS THE room was a door leading to other compartments in the cellar. The whole basement—which was a very large one, extending outward to the rear of the house, beneath the yard area—was partitioned off into rooms and used by various members of the rebel fraternity as dormitories during their frequent visits. Standing in the doorway was a man who certainly had not been there when Mark had come in.

Vaguely he remembered seeing him before. That gaunt, dour visage and....

Abruptly he remembered. This was the man who had occupied the cell next to him, and who had argued with Murf about his chances of escape. Later, when the prison break had been staged, he had been freed with the rest.

"How long have you been there?" Mark asked.

"Since you started to talk," said the man.

Murf frowned and glowered at him. But Smid motioned him to a seat.

"Sandy," he introduced. "He's one of the riders. Good man, even if his ancestry is mostly Mic. Born here, though. I knew him as a child."

Mark nodded. "Is it a habit of yours to eavesdrop?" he asked.

"I wasn't eavesdropping," denied Sandy. "I heard you come in and I headed this way. Anything this Mic has a hand in, I like to know about. So I stood there and listened. You could have seen me sooner if you'd looked up."

Murf growled, but his eyes twinkled. "He's suspicious of his own shadow. Thinks he's being followed."

Sandy's eyes were fixed balefully on the redhead. "I heard what I expected to hear," he said.

Mark could see the hate smoldering between the two men.

Sandy's was frank, as if he didn't care who knew about it, least of all Murf. Murf was calmly supercilious, confident that it couldn't hurt him.

"What did you expect to hear?" asked Mark.

"I expected to hear this Mic trying to veto any idea which might prevent his brother Mics from invading the country."

Smid was plainly uneasy. "Stop it," he said. "We have dispelled all doubt of Murf's allegiance. That has all been covered before and proven to be nothing but a lot of wild talk based on a shock of red hair. Let's have no more of it."

"I take more convincing than the rest of you," Sandy declared. "Smooth talk doesn't touch me. And right now I want to know something."

"What is it?" asked Mark, his eyes on Murf who was apparently completely at ease. A little chill coursed its way down Mark's spine. Murf seemed a little too much at ease considering he was being accused of the vilest treachery.

"I want to know what the twenty-first dispatch rider is for."

"The twenty…" Smid interrupted himself to stare at Murf. "I thought there were only twenty needed."

Murf grinned. "There are," he replied. "Suppose you call in the man that bothers you, Sandy."

Sandy left the room with a scowl. In a minute he was back with a man dressed in his underwear, who seemed a bit put, out about being awakened. He blinked his eyes and stared belligerently around the room.

"There are twenty of us," Sandy said. "And each man has his orders, covering every section of the duchy, three of them covering the other duchies. But there are twenty-one horses being kept in readiness down in the stable. I checked up and found that the odd horse had been assigned to this man. His name is Doog, another Mic! He won't tell us what his orders are. Very mysterious about it."

Mark looked at the man, who at that moment recognized

him and saluted belatedly. "Repeat your orders," said Mark, returning the salute.

The man looked bewildered. "I can't," he said.

"Why can't you?"

"I don't have any."

Mark looked at Murf who was grinning maliciously toward Sandy.

"What's it all about?"

"VERY SIMPLE," Murf claimed. "I've got twenty men with orders who must mobilize all our forces when the word is given. It would be a shame to get anybody confused by changing the orders at the last minute. And that is what would happen if one of our men should get sick or be injured. His sector would have to be covered by some of the others. It would spoil the timing, too."

"And so this man is to be given the orders of the man who gets sick, if any," finished Mark. "Commendable foresight. Satisfied, Sandy?"

"No, and I never will be. How about the extra horse? Both a horse and a man won't get sick at the same time."

"No, you lunkhead," said Murf. "But if either one got sick it would cause a lot of trouble. So I have an extra one of each."

"Then why is this guy so mysterious? Pretending he has orders and won't tell the rest of us what they are."

They all looked at the man, and he smirked self-consciously. "They all had their orders and I didn't. So I let on I did."

Mark laughed explosively. The others joined him, with the exception of Sandy. He glared at Murf, his suspicion not allayed in the least.

"You'll all realize I'm right, after it's too late," he growled.

With this dire prophecy he left the room, slamming the door after him. Mark chuckled and pretended not to see the glance which passed between Murf and the twenty-first rider.

"I bet he'll turn out to be a fighting fool when the time comes, suspicions or no suspicions," he said.

Murf nodded. "He's a fighter, all right," he admitted. "But he's annoying at times."

"Then everything's settled," Mark said. "I'll return to the prison and resume my work. The attack is postponed until we can install my machines. Understood?"

Murf nodded again.

Smid suddenly looked anxious. "But you're not going back to the prison? You'll have to perform in the arena again!"

"Safe as home in bed," said Mark, and they knew he wasn't boasting. "And it wouldn't serve any purpose to have all of Erlayok's men looking for me. As it is he knows where I am without knowing what I'm doing. If I didn't go back, the first place he would look is here. He already suspects Murf, and knows I'm connected with him. Besides, all my equipment is at the jail, and it's too cumbersome to move without attracting attention."

Mark sensed the next question before it came. "This equipment," queried Murf. "Where did you get it? And how can you work without the guards stopping you?"

"I told you that I used hypnotism to get out of there tonight. They leave me alone for the same reason. They fully believe that I am working on some machine which I shall use to entertain the crowd in the arena. As for the equipment, it consists of ordinary tools and hardware. Once I described it, they brought it to me."

Murf regarded him keenly. "This hypnotism," he said. "I've heard of it. Some kind of magic, isn't it? A powerful weapon for one who can use it?"

Smid was plainly awed. Mark, noticing his interest, coupled with Murf's question, was struck with a bright idea.

"Yes," he admitted. "Powerful in its way. Would you like to see it work?"

Without waiting for an answer Mark fixed his eyes on the

twenty-first rider, and exerted his will. The man's face showed that he was instantly under control.

"YOU ARE familiar," said Mark, calmly, "with the type of faithful dog who worshipfully follows his master wherever he goes. Suppose you, as a man, had that same regard for me, your master. In fact you *have* such an affection, haven't you?"

As he said this Mark rose and walked across the room. The man got up and followed, docilely.

"That's a good boy," said Mark, and then leaned over and whispered to Murf: "Try to stop him!"

Murf looked startled and then did as he was asked. As Mark walked past him, followed by the hypnotized man, he suddenly stepped between them and spoke sharply to Doog. But Doog merely stepped around him and continued following Mark. Murf grabbed his arm and tried to stop him. Doog snarled and slapped the hand away. Murf stepped back, alarm showing in his eyes.

Mark smiled and sat down. "Sit over there," he directed Doog, and turned to the others. "The show's over. Simple, isn't it?"

Doog was still in the hypnotic trance, though Murf and Smid didn't know it. They supposed that Mark's "show's over" had released him. Mark meant them to think that way. Murf seemed to be shaken by the exhibition.

He had never thought that one man could possibly exert such power over the will of another. The fact frightened him, hardheaded as he was. Smid was frankly admiring. In the course of their association Mark had astounded him time after time. His diversified talents had impressed Smid as much as his zeal as a patriot.

"The night must be drawing to an end," Mark hazarded. "I'd better be getting back to the prison. Suppose you two lead the way to the door. It's not safe to show a light upstairs and you know the way better than I."

Smid obligingly led the way, followed by Murf. Neither saw

Doog obediently rise and walk after Mark. At the front door Smid peered out and scanned the street.

"Night watch is elsewhere," he said.

"Okay," answered Mark. "I'll see you gentlemen after the games are over. I'll have the machines by then. Right now I'm going to run for a few blocks. If I'm seen on the streets, I don't want it to happen around here."

Murf nodded and Smid stepped aside. Mark suddenly darted out the door and ran down the street. He heard a slight commotion behind him but didn't turn his head. He knew that Doog in his haste to follow had bowled over the other two men. Mark didn't stop until he was around a corner two blocks away. Doog panted to his side.

A quick glance around the corner told him that Murf hadn't started to follow as yet.

"Doog!" he said. "What were Murf's orders?"

"Ride direct to Govern and inform him of rebellion."

"New orders," Mark snapped. "Remember this when you ride through York—remember at York—that you are to turn back and lend a hand to the first revolutionists you see fighting."

When Murf arrived at the corner he found Mark gravely passing his hands across Doog's face. He stopped and watched the mysterious process. Finally Mark gave a quick flourish and snapped his fingers. His lips were moving as he did this, no doubt mouthing some obscure incantations, Murf thought. With the snap, Doog's expression changed and he looked about him in bewilderment. Mark sighed in apparent relief.

"He was a tough customer," he breathed. "Thought he would never come out of it. Now you two get back under cover before somebody sees you."

CHAPTER XIX

BROTHER CAT

MARK DIDN'T IMMEDIATELY renew his attack on the problem when he returned to the prison. His mind was too filled with anger at Murf. Still he couldn't quite believe that the redhead was really a traitor. Yet could he doubt it? Govern was the commander-in-chief of the Mic forces and there could be only one reason for notifying him of the rebellion among the Brish. And that was to give the Mics an opportunity to stage an attack.

Mark realized that he should have suspected something long ago. Murf's frequent reference to the inhabitants of Scarbor, in which he labeled them a scary bunch, among other things, should have warned him weeks before. But the redhead's obvious sympathy for the down-trodden people, and his plans to relieve them of oppression, had stilled any vagrant suspicions before they had taken form, Mark shook his head and almost wished he hadn't discovered Murf's perfidy.

For Murf, whatever else he might be, he proved himself a friend.

Mark couldn't forget that. He was thinking of it, in fact, as he decided to defer any disposition he might make of Murf. There was nothing the man could do to harm the Brish, or interfere with his plans, now that Doog had been taken care of. And Doog wouldn't even know that his orders had been tampered with until he passed through the city of York.

And then the effect of Mark's post-hypnotic suggestion would drive him to aid the rebels. But there was no use in thinking further about the matter, for he didn't intend to give the word which would start the rebellion for some time.

And in the meantime....

Mark looked at his jumbled mass of apparatus, feeling suddenly disgusted with the whole setup. His efforts seemed to be frustrated at every turn. He continued to gaze at the diversified electrical equipment, and tried to concentrate on the problem of artificially creating the hypnosis wave. And at the same time trying to keep his mind from returning to the methods he knew were useless. It was while engaged in trying to think up a new approach that the sound of the morning gong beat in upon his consciousness.

And with the sound came a return of the idea which had been driven from his mind on the day previous.

Cursing softly at his own stupidity, his face revealed his glee as he viciously kicked all of the apparatus into a broken heap. The twinges of pain he experienced each time his sandaled toe came in contact with something heavy, seemed to stimulate his thought toward its logical conclusion.

The equipment, he knew, would be of no further use to him. The civilization which had designed it originally had not been far enough advanced to uncover the knowledge needed to create the short waves of thought by machinery. The apparatus of that civilization was too primitive!

On the face of it, this conclusion seemed more discouraging than otherwise. For it followed that Mark's knowledge of short-wave phenomena was of necessity insufficient to accomplish his purpose. But instead of feeling depressed, Mark was elated. For he knew now how he could obtain the necessary machines!

Omega had told him of a race of people on another planet that had managed to devise compact machines which controlled the sub-atomic energies which pervade all space. These machines manufactured the telekinetic wave, a second-cousin to the hypnosis wave. Omega had also said that when Mark had succeeded in making a machine to produce the hypnosis wave, he would be able to make adjustments on the same machine so that it would furnish its own power by means of the telekinesis wave. They were so near in frequency it was the same as producing two notes on a violin.

Therefore it would work both ways! Omega could copy the design of the telekinesis machine and he would do the rest. He should have thought of it long ago.

Perhaps the fact that Omega had said that this other race had no more intelligence than he, had made him go ahead with attempting to duplicate the feat without thinking that he might borrow the idea. But he realized, when he remembered that the device had been compact, that the knowledge of the race must have been superior to his own. Any apparatus of his that would come anywhere near the shortness of thought waves, would be decidedly bulky. Therefore, the methods of the other people were far more advanced.

He had forgotten, at the time that Omega had told the story, that intelligence and knowledge were two different things. Intelligence is the ability to solve new problems. And after all, Omega had only said that it lay within the mechanical genius of man to produce the waves. He hadn't said that Mark himself possessed sufficient knowledge.

THE ONLY thing necessary was to contact Omega. Mark groaned. He didn't know how to! Always in the past, Omega had come and gone of his own accord. He had never told Mark how he might be summoned in an emergency, though frequently he had opportunely appeared at such moments.

Casting back in his memory, he tried to think if he had at any time sent out an unconscious mental call for his benefactor? Thinking it over, he decided he hadn't.

But Mark was now in a state of mind where any straw was a redwood. He had to contact Omega and get the necessary information before it was too late. And if thinking about him might attract his attention, it wouldn't hurt to try it. He set about the task, concentrating on his ubiquitous friend to the exclusion of all else.

He became so absorbed in this pursuit that he only allowed

a small portion of his mind to notice and respond when Spud appeared with the manacles. Without speaking he allowed him to fasten them, and followed him into the guard room. He was still concentrating mightily when Chumly and Erlayok's man came to escort him to the arena for the third day's games. Both noticed his preoccupation, but forebore to intrude upon it. Chumly, out of courtesy, and Erlayok's man as a matter of policy.

But once within the prisoners' room under the stands, he was forced to give up his mental exercise. Several of the men who had survived the preceding days of performing, gathered around him as soon as he arrived. One of them, it seemed, had some news to impart. One of the guards was an obscure relative of his and had told him what he had learned of the program of today's games. And Mark, he had learned, was to head the day's bill by entering the arena to do battle with three lions!

Mark didn't feel any too optimistic about the prospect, even when told that he would be allowed to use his axe. Erlayok certainly was leaving no stone unturned to give him the works. The Earl had no doubt decided that it would be useless to try to force any information from him, and was therefore trying to get him killed. And if he should survive these games, Mark thought, Erlayok would probably do his utmost to have him assassinated. *If* he survived the games....

There was a certain amount of comfort in the thought of the axe. It might give him a chance. Erlayok had very likely allowed its use only because to give him a lesser weapon would have been obvious murder. And Mark had become popular with the spectators in the past two days. Although they were anxious to see him perform, the Earl nevertheless was obliged to extend him a fighting chance, however slim. The crowd would not have stood for less. And Mark began to formulate a plan to use that fighting chance.

It was likely that the beasts would be loosed one by one. Mark had learned that the lions were kept in individual cages, and that the system for releasing them was to roll the cage to the door opening on the pit, then to lift the cage door.

When the lion came out of the cage it had to walk directly into the arena, and the iron doors were slammed behind it. And inasmuch as the door was only wide enough to permit one cage to be rolled against it at a time, Mark was becoming hopeful as to the outcome of the battle.

His plan was simple. As each lion was released he would attack it and try to dispatch it before another could be loosed. If only they didn't turn all three lions out, and then send him last!

BUT NOTHING of the sort happened. Mark was given his axe and the barred door to the arena was held open. He stepped immediately to the door behind which the animals were all kept. Even if he hadn't known which one it was, his nose would have told him. The booming sounds of the announcer's voice mingled with the snarls of the beasts within.

A cage was being wheeled toward the door. Mark felt an inward qualm as he faced the animal through the bars.

This lion was massive, black-maned, and apparently not as well starved as the one he had battled before. But that fact gave him no satisfaction whatever.

This beast looked far more formidable, and every bit as ferocious.

The iron-barred door was swung inward, and the cage rolled against the opening. Mark gripped his axe tightly as a man climbed to the top of the cage. As the door rattled from his fumblings with the catch, the king of beasts crouched and fixed his eyes balefully on Mark. He appeared to know just what was going on. And the crouch indicated that he intended to spring as soon as the door was lifted.

Mark, knowing that the weight of the animal would bowl him over, stepped aside and prepared to get in an axe-cut as he flashed past.

The cage-door lifted, and Mark swung savagely. The axe bit deeply into the shoulder of the lion as he sprang forth with a tremendous leap. But surprisingly the lion paid no heed. Mark had expected, little though he knew of the habits of lions, that the beast would wheel and return the attack ferociously. But it didn't. It simply let the rules go hang.

When the leap ended the beast continued its progress toward the center of the pit, running proudly, its head carried high. Mark, frantic at the lost seconds, sprang in pursuit. If he didn't catch and vanquish this animal instantly, he would have to face three of them.

He caught it, all right, but as he aimed a crippling blow at the animal's spine, it suddenly wheeled and crouched. But it didn't crouch as the other lion had. This might be considered half a crouch. The fore-quarters went down, but the rear remained up, the tail waving on high.

That way the beast looked well, actually friendly. Like a household pet. And the idea of a lion romping about the house—anybody's house—was definitely disconcerting. It didn't make sense.

Mark stopped his axe blow and hesitated, confused. The unorthodox behavior of the animal stunned him for a moment. But he was too intent on the work to be done to hesitate long.

He aimed a terrific blow at the beast's head, hoping to cleave the skull. But the lion dodged and jumped aside like a playful kitten. It then took up its ridiculous stance in a new spot, meanwhile turning loose a half-hearted roar, reproachful in tone.

It was like a magnified meow from a loyal but much-put-upon tabby. Even the face looked hurt and reproachful—which is an interesting way for any lion's face to be.

But Mark was too busy to notice any of this. All he knew was that he had missed. The axe had buried itself in the ground.

Savagely he wrenched it loose and aimed another cut. The lion repeated its antic. This time Mark saw the silliness of the beast's maneuver, and pulled the axe from the dirt slowly.

He now had a definite feeling that this encounter was entering a new phase: a phase in which he would find the axe of no value whatever. And he was quite right.

The expression on the lion's face distinctly said "Hiya, sucker."

It came happily over to lick at Mark's hand. Mark, his eyes glinting, kicked the lion square in the stomach. Tears welled from its eyes as it sat back on its haunches and raised a paw to its belly. "Now is that nice?" Mark swore later he heard a voice say.

The crowd roared its approval. The lion eyed them thoughtfully. Mark sneaked up and cuffed its moth-eaten ears.

"I hope you're feeling this," chortled Mark, giving a final cuff. "If you're going to be a lion, you might try to be a good one. Come on, let's show these yokels a good fight."

"You asked for it, pal," said the lion in the voice of Omega, eyeing the two beasts which had just entered the pit. He gave a tremendous roar and started toward them, Mark at his side. The two newcomers saw the impending attack and crouched, waiting to spring.

But both Mark and Omega executed the move which would nullify the advantage of the springing attack. As if they had done this thing often, they veered away from each other and came toward the two lions from an angle. The lions sprang just the same, but the effectiveness of the leaps was gone.

CHAPTER XX

HASTY REBEL

MARK DODGED THE raking claws of his adversary, and dealt a blow which ended his half of the performance. His axe caught the beast in the center of the backbone, severing it. The lion thudded to the ground, thrashed for a moment and was still.

But Omega was giving the crowd its money's worth. These people had never seen a battle between two lions before.

Omega bit and he clawed. He also snarled, between bites. All in all it was a sight worth seeing, and everybody present, including Mark, was enjoying it.

The battle was foreordained to go the way it did. Omega, the larger lion, won. After about five minutes of swift and savage conflict, during which the ground became splattered with gore, the smaller beast gave up the ghost. The black-maned survivor gave a mighty roar and stepped mincingly toward Mark.

"Pretty good for the mangy shape I'm in," he said. "What did you want to see me about?"

The crowd was watching them curiously, fascinated by what appeared to be a completely novel relationship between lion and man. The situation was, for the moment, just a little bit embarrassing.

"Walk on your hind legs, or something," Mark suggested. "I can't take a lion back into the prisoners' room with me. You'd scare people. And I've some things to talk about. Do some tricks here, while I talk to you."

"Just a few simple tricks, I suppose," the lion said scathingly. "Like sawing a nitwit in half."

"Call your own shots, but get busy."

Omega obligingly treated the crowd to a series of antics which no self-respecting lion would have done, while Mark explained his inability to manufacture the hypnosis wave.

"I thought you were a bit over-confident," Omega remarked, between nipups. "What do you want me to do about it?"

"Keep moving," Mark told him. "Make it faster and funnier; give 'em their money's worth. What're we here for?"

Omega reared on his hind legs and went into a bowdler-ized hula, and Mark explained that he could use the plans of the machine already developed by the race of beings of which Omega had spoken. At this point the lion dropped to all fours and snarled menacingly. The stands suddenly shouted in unison. It appeared that the beast had suddenly decided to turn savage, and refuse to obey further the commands of his conqueror.

Even Mark, surprised by the change, went instinctively on his guard for a second—then grinned. "Give," he said.

"Didn't I tell you those people were destroyed when their sun exploded?" the lion growled.

"Sure, sure," answered Mark aiming a kick at the beast's nose. "What of it? It happened during your lifetime. So you can travel back and take a look at the machines for me."

The lion crouched, dodging the kick. Then he leaped on Mark, bearing him to the ground. They tussled, rolled back and forth in mock combat. Omega growled and snarled his reply. "Ungrateful whelp! You know what trouble I've had with time. It isn't fair to ask! I won't do it!"

"You've got to," Mark told him. "You got me into all this. You should have known that I don't have enough knowledge to invent the necessary machinery. You certainly knew that the race you spoke of was further advanced than my own. And yet you encouraged me. Told me to go ahead. Now I've wasted half the week, and the rebellion might fail due to the delay. It's your moral obligation to provide these machines."

The lion sat back on his haunches and panted dejectedly. "How could I know you would fall down on the job?" he wailed. "You were so cocky about it."

"You should have known," said Mark uncompromisingly.

"Why should I? I don't know anything about machinery. All I've ever done is copy things already invented. I've got no use for it myself."

"But you realize your responsibility, don't you? Think of the endless wars which the machines will prevent. You've always said you're against wars. Here's your chance to do something about it."

"I know," Omega admitted. "I might have known I'd have no peace of mind once I dabbled in human affairs. It's easy to start, but then you can't stop. All right, I'll do it. So long!"

Mark grinned. "Phooey!" he said. "You're enjoying yourself."

THEN ABRUPTLY he realized that Omega had already left. The lion remained, to be sure, but then Omega had only usurped the body of a lion already in existence. He hadn't created this beast. Mark had been fooled, expecting the lion to vanish when

Omega left. He realized his mistake when the beast suddenly crouched and prepared to leap.

Frantically Mark snatched out his axe.

The crowd came to its feet and roared as the lion unleashed the spring-steel muscles in its long body. Mark dodged sideways and lashed out with the axe. It landed, but not fatally.

The lion wheeled and returned to the attack. Its mouth was open, revealing sharp, yellow fangs. There followed a series of rushes, Mark dodging agilely and getting in a number of axe-cuts. Once he slipped in a puddle of gore, and almost went down. That time he only escaped the slashing talons by a hair's-breadth.

After a few minutes of this game of cat and mouse, the lion showed signs of tiring. It had lost quite a bit of blood, and its rushes weren't as swift as at first. Mark noticed this and set himself for the kill.

Remembering the ease with which one blow had dispatched the other lion, he waited for the beast to make another attack. Then he dodged aside and brought the axe down in the center of the animal's spine.

The battle ended.

BACK IN the room with the other prisoners Mark listened, embarrassed, to the praise which invariably came after one of his performances. This time even the guards were voluble.

One of them suggested that, inasmuch as it was certain he would survive the games, he should join up with the army of his master, one of the lesser nobles. The idea immediately took hold. There were members of several of these forces, and they all presented arguments why he should associate himself with them. Among the guards were a few of Erlayok's men. They kept a strict silence, knowing the Earl's enmity for Mark.

But to all this, the prisoners had only amused smiles. Mark was aware that they, to a man, knew that he was the rebel leader, and would have nothing to do with the armies of the nobles. Several, in fact, were members of his own gang of patriots, condemned to the games for that and other reasons.

Some of these had been subjected to torture, and bore the scars, but none of them had revealed any but the vaguest information. They had been sentenced to the games because they had convinced their captors that they knew nothing of value.

An unexpected commotion at the street entrance put a stop to all discussion.

A man, it seemed, was trying to get in. The guards at the gate were pushing him away, probably thinking him demented, but each time he insisted on coming back.

He succeeded in gaining admittance finally, when he reached through the bars and tweaked the nose of one of Erlayok's men. The one, in fact, who was assigned to keep a watch on Mark, and who didn't like the job a bit. He opened the gate and yanked the offender inside.

Then he knocked him to the floor with his fist.

Mark looked at the wizened figure of the man and gave a start. It was Smid, but an almost unrecognizable Smid. He was covered with dried blood from a wound on the scalp, and his hands, clothes and face were caked with filth. Seeing Mark, he scurried over to him.

The guards laughed and made no move to interfere. It struck them funny that anyone would try to break into such a place.

"He's done it!" Smid gasped, almost falling again.

Mark reached out a hand and steadied him, "Calm yourself," he said. "Who did what?"

"Murf!" said Smid. "He sent off the dispatch riders!"

Mark's eyes narrowed. "You mean with the mobilization orders? Or the new orders?"

Smid shook his head, impatiently; grabbed Mark's arm and talked fast.

"The original orders. Our men to converge within the city inside of an hour! He fought a duel with Sandy after you left, and killed him. The riders knew nothing of the new orders from you, and Murf killed Sandy before he could tell them. When I tried to stop him, he hit me over the head and left me for dead."

Mark felt his plans crashing about his ears. The premature attack might well ruin everything. Doog, of course, would never deliver his message to Govern, but that made little difference, now.

The big thing was to see that the initial steps in the rebellion were carried through, now that it was started.

If the Mics saw their opportunity and crossed the border while the Brish were at odds, there would be a better chance to repel them if he had the reigns firmly in his hands, here in Scarbor. If only this could have been delayed until Omega returned with the machines....

CHAPTER XXI

THE SENTIMENTAL AUTOCRAT

MARK FIXED HIS eyes on the nearest of the guards. The man stiffened. Mark repeated the process rapidly—giving none a chance to realize what was happening—until all the soldiers in the room were under his control. All but one. Chumly, sensing immediately that something was wrong, looked expectantly toward Mark. He displayed his good sense by making no attempt to interfere.

"Chumly," said Mark. "Go at once to Jon, your master, and tell him to get his family to a safe place. Don't delay."

Chumly obeyed at once, without question. He left by the street gate. The guards, still in the hypnotic trance, Mark sent into the arena to do pitched battle for the edification of the crowd. He figured that this unexpected addition to the program, would keep the nobles puzzled for a while.

The attack would have already started before they would realize that the prisoners had been released, and that they had a rebellion on their hands.

One of the soldiers was in charge of Mark's stainless-steel

axe, and Mark relieved him of it before he sent him out. Then, hastily giving orders to the other prisoners, he sent them forth to obtain weapons. He took a last look across the arena, and had the satisfaction of seeing Jon hurriedly leave his box.

Erlayok was still seated, apparently unperturbed at the unusual battle going on in the pit.

Across the street several horses were tethered outside a drinking house. Mark untied two of them, and he and Smid rode off. In a few minutes, they pulled up in front of the haberdashery shop.

Leaving hasty instructions for the men who remained there, they immediately departed for Mark's prison. Some time ago Mark had decided to make the prison his headquarters during the attack. He half suspected that Erlayok knew that Smid's house was a meeting place of the rebels. The man had too many spies not to know it. He had probably left it alone for the reason that as long as there were rebels it was best to know where he could lay his hands on them, whereas if he raided the place they would only find a new headquarters he might not be able to discover.

But that reason wouldn't stop him once the rebellion was under way. It would be the first place he would think to crush in a belated attempt to stop the rebels. And Mark, for a while at least, wanted lines of communication kept open.

Even with the swiftness with which his forces would strike, there was always the possibility that certain bands would be repulsed and require reïnforcements. It was imperative that all the strategic points be taken, and it must be known immediately if any of the scattered forces needed help.

THE MEN who remained at Smid's would inform all contact riders of the change of headquarters. In the event of an attack on the old headquarters, they would leave safely by means of a passage into the adjoining houses.

By passing word at the last moment, Mark made certain that the information wouldn't be carried by spies to any of the nobles.

*Mark's axe slashed out like something
alive and malevolent*

Already the streets were filled with groups of armed men. These were the vanguard of the rebel forces which would shortly take the city. They were carefully nonchalant in their movements, talking quietly as they walked. No two groups seemed to be traveling in the same direction, and no group paid any attention to any of the others.

In a matter of minutes these scattered groups would converge in a dozen places at the same time. The strongholds of the various nobles would be simultaneously attacked, and each would be too busy to help the other.

Mark hoped fervently that his men would find the going easy. He hoped that the palaces would fall without too much bloodshed.

On the way to the prison Mark commandeered the services of several rebels. These were to be Smid's bodyguard, for Mark had no intention of remaining at the prison headquarters. He had a job to do himself, and it would take him elsewhere. Smid would issue the necessary orders should any of his compatriots need reïnforcements.

When he got to the prison Mark summoned the four guards and the captain, who had his office on the street side of the building. Briefly he told them of the sudden turn of affairs.

"The point is this," he concluded. "Are you going to help us— or do I tuck you all in a cell?"

The four guards were converted immediately, but, the captain blustered and refused to understand that there would shortly be a change of authority. Mark wasted no time in ordering him into a cell.

"You can put these men to work, Smid," Mark said. "Send them out to commandeer fresh horses for the riders as they come in. And keep riders coming and going between here and every point of attack you can. The more reports you have, the more certain will be our success. I'm leaving now. See you later."

Mark remounted and left the courtyard at a gallop. Already the din of a dozen battles could be heard from all quarters of the city. Mark rode furiously toward the palace of Erlaken, a lesser noble. Mark was relieved that modern feudal England was different from the England of ancient feudal times, when the lords had maintained their castles on their own lands, scattered all over the country. Such a condition would have made the present rebellion impossible.

Today, with all the nobles banded together, their strongholds situated in only four key cities of the whole nation, it was far simpler to strike them all at once. And yet the nobles had no doubt banded together originally for their own protection. Any attack by foreigners was easier defended against this way.

The nobles could surround themselves with their combined armies instead of scattering their forces all over the countryside. With the present system it was impossible for an enemy to defeat them, one by one. They had probably never considered the weakness in case of an attack from within.

THE PALACE of Erlaken was already in the rebels' hands

when Mark arrived. Several hundred had forced the gates by storm before the handful of defenders could make out what was going on. A cheer went up as Mark rode through the gates to congratulate the captain of the rebels. Nothing had been destroyed, and the rebels were locking all the earl's men in the dungeons.

Everything had been done on schedule, and the rebels were ready to repel any attempts to retake the palace. The earl himself, it was planned, would be taken prisoner by those assigned to attack the soldiers and nobles at the arena.

Mark rode forth to visit the next nearest castle. He hoped the rebels had done as well there. As he galloped through the streets, his mind returned to Murf. Almost all of this had been planned by the redhead. Even to the course Mark was now taking to lend his moral support to the attackers.

All the elaborate timetable of the rebel forces, that their attacks would be simultaneous and unexpected, had been of his devising. He had worked for days on the timing, studying the distances to be covered and figuring the speeds which could be expected over the various available routes.

No detail had been overlooked, that the small rebel forces would be able to cover all the necessary points, and accomplish the work of a much larger body of fighters. It had taken military genius of the first water to do all this, and a tremendous amount of labor.

And yet the redhead was a traitor. It didn't make sense.

Mark reached his destination and again found the work already done. Things were going even better than planned. There was no doubt of it, the absence of so many of the defenders, who might otherwise have been there to fight if it weren't for the games, was responsible for the ease with which these two captures had been made.

Yet in the end it didn't matter much, for those same soldiers were still to be reckoned with. A good many of them would band together in an effort to retake their strongholds.

This castle had been taken without a casualty on either side, due to the fact that the gates had been open to admit a tradesman's cart. The rebels had rushed in and forced the defenders to surrender. The thing had been done in an orderly fashion. No pillage, no destruction. Discipline had been admirable. Each rebel detachment was under the leadership of an officer who had orders from Murf, Smid and Mark, to allow no rioting.

Further, it had been impressed upon all the rebels that for the time being everything captured was to be considered government property. And they had been told that under the new system of government every citizen would own his share of the state's wealth. And if that wealth were destroyed or stolen, each citizen would suffer by the taxation necessary to replace it.

HERE AGAIN Mark was forced to think of Murf. For although it was Mark who had suggested that these things be impressed upon their men, it was Murf who got the idea of holding the officers of each group personally responsible for the conduct of his men.

It was he, also, who had decreed that any deaths which occurred, over and above those necessary in the course of the fighting, would be considered murder and the killers treated as such. This idea of Murf's would save many an innocent life.

Mark growled to himself as he rode off to his next point of call.

Twice on the way he lent his flashing axe to groups of rebels who had been attacked on the streets by bands of soldiers returning to their respective castles. Each time a rebel victory resulted.

These delays irked him, for although he fought with the fury of one possessed, several valuable minutes were lost on each occasion. These skirmishes had not been figured in the timing of his rounds. He feared the consequences of the departure from his carefully prearranged schedule. But his fears were groundless.

When he arrived at his destination he found the situation already in hand. The surprise element had again proved its worth.

There remained only one really important spot to be visited.

Erlayok's castle. This stronghold was always overrun with soldiers, even during the games, and its walls were high—practically unscalable.

All other points of attack consisted of garrisons of soldiers and public buildings, and sufficient men had been allotted to these places to ensure their capture.

As Mark's speeding horse neared the castle of Erlayok, he sensed that there was trouble ahead.

There was altogether too much noise for the place to have been taken. His fears were realized when he came in sight of the castle. Not only had it not been taken, but from the looks of things it was doubtful if it would be.

The tops of the walls were lined with archers, pouring arrows down on the unprotected men who were trying to batter down the oaken gates with a heavy ram. Men were darting out from the cover of nearby buildings to take the places of their fallen comrades at the ram.

Mark pulled up and dismounted, leaving the horse out of arrow range.

He ran forward ignoring the flying shafts. He saw that occasionally a soldier would fall from the wall, a victim of a rebel arrow, but not often. Not nearly often enough. The few rebels who could handle a bow were no match for the archers of the earl.

As he neared the ram, his heart sank as he saw the rebels drop it and run for cover. The punishment had been too much for them.

Savagely Mark broke the shaft of an arrow which had gone clear through the biceps of his left arm. He retreated as he pulled the broken bits from his flesh.

The situation looked hopeless at first. The rebels had been unable to install any siege machinery in the vicinity before the attack. And the ram would never break through without some sort of contraption to protect the men as they plied it, Mark didn't waste time trying to invent an alternate plan but gave immediate orders to start construction of a huge bulwark to shield the ram.

But in another portion of the city, events had taken place which would shortly solve the problem of the siege of Erlayok's castle.

At the very instant that the perfectly timed attacks of the rebels were begun at the gates of the four castles of the reigning nobles, an entirely different scene was being enacted before still another great palace.

A compact force of two hundred men gathered at the castle of Jon, Duke of Scarbor. They made no attempt to cross the bridge over the moat. The soldiers stationed there stared at them in alarm, but seeing that no attack was forthcoming, made no move to raise the bridge.

In a few minutes the Duke appeared. Without hesitation he singled out the two rebel leaders and beckoned them to him. They saluted and bowed stiffly.

"Explain this, please," demanded the Duke.

One of the captains bowed again and answered. "There is a rebellion in progress," he said. "We have been sent here to see that I no harm comes to you or your family."

"Does anyone wish us harm?" inquired the Duke.

THE CAPTAIN looked embarrassed. "Not many," he answered. "But there is a small group among us who think that no noble should be left to live, lest there some day be a return of the sort of government we have been subjected to."

"Then the majority wish my family well?"

"Oh, of course," replied the captain. "Mark, our leader, and Murf, his lieutenant gave orders that you were to be protected. In fact they don't want any of the nobles killed, just removed from power. But there are many who would like to see all aristocrats dead, so it was thought advisable that you be guarded from harm."

Jon stroked a clean-shaven chin. "Very civilized sort of a revolt," he remarked.

He was interrupted by the clatter of a horseman who dismounted breathlessly. He saluted briskly, bowed briefly to the Duke.

"Orders from Smid, at headquarters: If no disturbance in vicinity of Duke's palace, dispatch one company to castle of Erlayok. Answer."

The two captains looked at each other. "That means you," said one. "They must be having trouble over there." He turned to the horseman. "Answer to Smid: All quiet here. Sending company immediately."

The dispatch rider mounted and galloped off.

"Just a minute," said Jon, as the second captain turned to address his men. "If there is trouble at Erlayok's palace, it can mean only one thing. His expert archers are preventing an attack on the gates. Do you have any archers to shoot them off the walls?"

The answer was obvious. All two hundred rebels were men from the farm lands, and there wasn't a bow among them. Some were armed with swords, a few had regular battle axes and the rest had woodcutting axes from their own farms.

The captains looked at each other and shook their heads. "But orders are orders," replied one. "Whether we can help or not."

"Yes," said the Duke. "But it would be much better if you had some archers. Suppose I lend you some. Will you make use of them?"

"You mean you would help our side to overthrow your own government?" said one, incredulously.

"It's not my government, as you well know," replied Jon. "And if my people want a change badly enough to fight for it, I shall certainly help them."

CHAPTER XXII

THE HAPPY REBEL

MARK WATCHED SKILLED carpenters hammer together a long, narrow shield from pieces of wood of all shapes and sizes garnered from doors, sheds and a dozen other sources in the neighborhood.

The work was progressing speedily, for the castle of Erlayok had to be taken before any help could arrive from the scattered soldiery about the city.

There were no wheels available and the shield wasn't to be made like the conventional article. It wouldn't be a self-supported canopy to be rolled to the door, while men walked safely underneath. There wasn't time for that, nor material.

When this contrivance was completed it would resemble a wooden roof, torn from a house. It would take a hundred men to carry it to the gates. But cumbersome and unwieldy as it might be, there would be safety beneath it for the men at the ram.

Aside from the importance of this last stronghold as a strategic place for either side to hold, Mark had another reason for wanting to get inside as quickly as possible.

He had just heard that Erlayok had left the arena in time to get here before the attack. He must have been warned by the unorthodox behavior of some of his own soldiers in the battle Mark had ordered. Further, he must have recognized that they were under hypnotic influence, and had jumped to the conclusion that Mark was behind it.

But whatever had warned him, he had left the arena before the rebels had blocked his escape, and was now inside. And Erlayok was the man who had to be destroyed.

A dispatch rider had informed Mark that the lesser nobles

and their families were in custody. The rest of the spectators at the arena had been allowed to return to their homes.

The only deaths at the arena had been caused by a few soldiers who had shown fight. These had been few and were evenly divided on both sides. Most of the soldiers had immediately offered their swords in behalf of the rebel cause, upon being informed that the nobles could no longer pay for their services. And best of all, no civilian, man, woman or child, had been harmed in any way.

Mark was beginning to feel easier in his mind. He wondered if the distant cities in the other duchies were doing as Scarbor.

The great shield was almost finished when a commotion rose from another side of the castle wall. Shouts were heard and the sound of marching feet. Mark dashed to the corner of the wall to see what it was all about.

Two hundred men, half of them archers in the uniforms of Jon's little forces, were tramping in marching order down the street. At their head, marching side by side, were the rebel captain and Jon, Duke of Scarbor.

MARK GRINNED and realized that he wasn't very surprised. Something had told him that the Duke was more interested in the welfare of his people than in the continuance of his own government. It was when Mark realized that the Duke had burned his bridges behind him and was throwing in with the rebels, that he made up his mind that Jon was the man to head the new government.

Murf was definitely out, even if Mark still did feel a vagrant and undeniable affection for the redhead. His treachery had proved that however much he might have sympathized with the oppressed population of England, he still owed his chief allegiance to the Mics, their foe.

And from what Mark had learned of Jon's father, Aired, the present king, it seemed likely that with advancing years he had weakened considerably in his efforts in behalf of his people.

Lately he had come to accept the domination of the nobles, and had lost much of his force. So Jon it would be.

The Duke returned Mark's grin. "I heard you needed some archers." Mark waved.

Jon's bowmen were deployed in the upper windows and on the roofs of the buildings across the street. It took them about three minutes to clear the walls of Erlayok's men. Every bolt loosed sped to its mark in the body of one of the defenders.

Mark rushed with a gang of his men to get the ram in action. Jon dashed forward with them, and though Mark waved him back he insisted on helping. Stepping over the bodies of arrow-pierced rebels, they picked up the ram where it had fallen.

A horde of rebel fighters crowded through the broken gates, the instant they succumbed to the battering blows of the heavy ram.

Mark went in with them, looking for Erlayok. As he had expected, the earl was not to be seen. The hand-to-hand fighting in the castle yard was violent and brief. Mark dashed into the castle, leaving mopping-up operations to his men.

Taking the stairs three at a time he burst into the corridor of Erlayok's private quarters. It was deserted and he went into the room where he had been chained a few days before. That was empty too. Frantically he searched every room on that floor but with no more success. Twice he saw frightened servants, but paid them no heed.

For some incomprehensible reason there was no one of importance in the whole castle. A thorough search, moreover, revealed no member of Erlayok's retinue, and very few of the surviving soldiers remained. There had been hundreds of the latter inside the walls, when the rebels had made their assault. But now, aside from the dead there was only a pitiful handful—those who had put up the losing fight in the castle yard.

THE ANSWER to the mystery was supplied when one of the rebels found a passage, leading from the torture chamber beneath the castle, under the street and emerging in the cellar of a house a block away. But it was too late.

Erlayok was gone.

Mark encountered Jon some time later. The Duke was marshaling his men for the return to his own palace. Mark thanked him for the valuable assistance his men had given. But the Duke shook his head, smiling.

"Don't thank me," he said. "I've been a part of this rebellion for years. Rather I should thank you."

Marked looked at him incredulously. "I don't understand."

"You have forgotten that the forces of law have been under my command," the Duke reminded. "A thousand times I have suppressed evidence which might have broken up the movement. I realized it was the only way my people would ever gain their freedom. It was little enough to do for them. My men have trailed you and the other leaders in almost all of your organizing work. We've protected your members dozens of times.

"We've prevented raids on your headquarters, making all sorts of excuses to those who demanded that they be made. Time after time your activities have been reported to me by various nobles, but always my investigations proved that they had been misinformed. So you see, I've really had a hand in this all the time."

"I see," Mark said. "That's what you meant when you said you weren't entirely uninformed."

"Yes," said Jon. "And part of my information concerns you. I have been told, for instance, that you never eat. What kind of man are you?"

"It's a little too complicated to go into right now. I've got to trace Erlayok."

"I hope you get him," said Jon. "He's the real reason for things being so bad. The other nobles don't dare offend him. And he's given me plenty of trouble with his spies. They have been so diligent in uncovering rebel activities that it's kept me busy covering up."

The two men shook hands and Mark mounted and rode off toward headquarters.

Perversely, Mark's thoughts strayed to Murf. He wondered if Jon knew anything of Murf's treachery. No, or he would have let the fact be known. Murf had gone about his job with such a thoroughness that his zeal had fooled everyone. Everyone, that is, except poor Sandy.

Mark urged the horse from a trot to a gallop. There were few people on the streets. Those who weren't actively engaged in the fighting were staying safely in their houses. And in this section of the city the fighting seemed to be over.

Approaching an intersection, his horse decided to show a mind of its own. It slowed its pace. Mark urged it on with a dig of his heels. The horse responded momentarily and then slowed again. Reaching the corner, it turned left. Mark pulled its head around and tried to make it turn back, but the animal continued in the new direction.

THEN SUDDENLY he forgot the horse's recalcitrance, and let it have its head. A block away he saw a shock of flaming red hair. At the sound of the horse's approach, Murf turned. For an instant it appeared that he would make an attempt to escape, but instead he stood his ground and grinned impishly.

Mark dismounted. Let Smid take care of the tracing of Erlayok. He would have already started on it by now, anyway. "Where have you been?" he asked, quietly.

Murf waved a hand, airily. "Where I was supposed to have been," he replied. "Leading the attack on the armory, as we planned I would."

Mark said nothing for a minute.

By his calculations Murf had finished his job of stirring up a revolt, and should be well on the way to meet the Mics which would be invading the country if Doog's message had gone through. Yet here he was aiding the rebellion. And though Murf didn't know that Doog would never deliver the message, it still didn't make sense.

He shouldn't be staying here and helping the rebels get control of the country. For the quicker order was restored, the quicker the Brish would be able to repel any attacks from the Mics. As far as that went, why had Murf planned the rebellion so well in the beginning? A poorly managed revolt would have served the purpose of the invaders a lot better.

"In case you're interested," Mark drawled. "Doog never got there."

Murf started guiltily. "Doog... You mean he was stopped?"

"Yes. I stopped him. I'm very much afraid your Mic army won't even know about our little shindig until it's too late to do them any good."

Murf bit his lip, muttering to himself.

"Come on, Murf," said Mark. "Let's have the whole story. I've nothing against you personally. And what's more I intend to give you a chance to escape."

"Escape! I don't want to escape. I want to see this revolt succeed! I want to see the new government in operation. But now... Oh, you won't believe me anyway."

He gestured hopelessly.

"Let's hear it just the same," Mark requested. "What comes after 'But now'?"

"But now you've spoiled it all!" Murf exploded.

"Calm yourself. How?"

Murf sighed.

"Well, listen, then. You won't believe me, but it's too late to matter now. If Doog had carried his message, here is what would have happened:

"Riders would have left Govern's headquarters and contacted all Mic and Mac commanders along the western and northern borders of this country. On all fronts a series of brief and ineffectual raids would have taken place. Little life would have been lost, but the Brish armies would have had their hands so full that none of them would have dared leave the borders unguarded for a minute.

"It would be made to appear that the country was in imminent danger of a massed invasion. The commanders of the Brish armies would have ignored a summons from any noble who might manage to get a message from one of the cities. As it is some noble is sure to get out of one of the cities, and will have no trouble dragging away a large force to fight the rebels."

"One already has, I greatly fear!" replied Mark. "But let's hear some more. How do you know Govern would do all this, instead of waiting a day or two and then invading after some of the Brish armies were removed?"

"Who has escaped?"

"Erlayok. But he might still be inside the city. Suppose you answer my question."

"Gladly. Govern would have done as I said because I ordered him to."

Mark shoved back his battered helmet and scratched his head. "Elucidate, my friend. This is getting screwier and screwier."

"NO DOUBT," grinned Murf. "There are a lot of things you don't know. In fact there are a lot of things none of the Brish know. Except, perhaps, Erlayok and a few army generals. I'll explain:

"I am Murf, second son of Rever, King of Eire, by his second wife, Ann Murfy. The plan to overthrow the despotic rule of Erlayok and his nobles originated in the council chambers of my father. And with the full knowledge of the ruler of the Macs. Not with the idea of conquest.

"But because we Mics and the Macs as well, are sick of the continual fighting on the borders.

"The British will tell you that their armies are purely defensive equipment. They believe it because Erlayok wants them to believe it. He couldn't make them pay taxes so readily otherwise. But the truth of the matter is that Erlayok has made repeated attempts to invade our territory, and has actually succeeded in grabbing a few small pieces.

"And though we can stop him by keeping eternally vigilant,

the expense has raised our taxes so that we are little better off than the Brish. We want to stop it! We don't want our people to suffer as the Brish have suffered. And the best way to stop it is to set up a government here which will consider the welfare of the people."

"Pretty, smart," Mark commented. "A puppet government to pay tribute to the Mics, and the Macs."

Murf's face became as red as his hair. "No!" he shouted. "A government which will give us peace by disbanding its armies!"

Mark looked at the redhead quizzically. If Murf was telling the truth… He decided to find out.

Murf became suddenly calm as Mark's eyes bored into his own. He relaxed visibly. Mark hesitated and then began to question him, certain that under the influence of hypnosis he would tell the truth.

Bit by bit, Mark extracted the story. Several times rebels passed along the street, but it looked to them as if Mark and Murf were carrying on an ordinary conversation.

Sandy, he learned, had been killed in a perfectly legitimate duel, which Sandy himself had started. Murf had hit Smid to stop him from telling the dispatch riders of the changed orders. He had done it in good faith, genuinely afraid that if Mark's machines were installed, the rebellion would be impossible, due to interference from the armies.

He considered his own plan of keeping them busy, a mere practical one. But he didn't dare tell of it without revealing his connection with the Mics, realizing that no Brish would believe it possible for a Mic to be anything but an enemy.

As an inspiration Mark asked about the status quo of the Brish borders, and was surprised to learn that they had been approximately the same for hundreds of years, except for the times when the Brish had grabbed a bit of land here and there. Erlayok's story of continual invasion from the west was a lie.

Satisfied, Mark released the redhead from his trance.

"I owe you an apology," he said. "You should have told me,

and this would never have happened. I'm not Brish, you know. Get up on that horse. You and Smid are going to shake hands!"

CHAPTER XXIII

THREE DAYS OF DOUBT

BACK AT HEADQUARTERS Smid jumped up from his seat at the table when he caught sight of Murf. Mark motioned him down again and dismissed several rebel dispatch riders from the room. Smid's eyes were gleaming murderously and a hand involuntarily raised to caress the spot where Murf had broken the scalp.

Mark told him the whole story, not forgetting to mention the hypnotic trance which guaranteed its truth. As he talked he saw the hard expression leave Smid's eyes to be replaced by one of incredulity.

"But..." He started to object, and was silenced by Mark.

"I've told you it's all true," Mark stated. "Propaganda by Erlayok notwithstanding. The Brish have been fooled for years. I can see that now. Nobody has a kick coming about the distribution of land. The Mics and the Macs don't want any more. And the Brish have all they need. The borders can remain as they are and the armies disbanded."

Smid nodded. "If you believe, then I can," he said, and turned to Murf. "Forget the bump on the head. It was included in your philosophy: No one man can stand in the way of the cause."

Murf stretched out his hand and Smid took it.

"Now that that's settled," said Mark, "what's the latest news?"

It was pretty nearly all good, according to Smid. The city was completely in the hands of the rebels.

Furthermore, their ranks has been swelled considerably by citizens whom they had been leery about approaching before, not to mention a good many soldiers who had no great love for the nobles.

News had come in from the duchy to the west that everything was under control. And best of all, there had been few unnecessary deaths and practically no wanton destruction of property.

But on the other side of the ledger was the fact that Erlayok, the most dangerous of the rebels, had escaped completely. No rider brought any word of him.

"There is one thing certain," said Smid. "The earl will send immediately for his entire forces at the border."

"Have Erlaken and Erlahul brought here at once," ordered Mark. "There is still a chance to checkmate him."

Under his direction Smid prepared official orders for the entire armies of the two earls to proceed under forced march to Scarbor. Completed, the orders only awaited the signatures of Erlaken and Erlahul to make them authentic. Smid already had the necessary seals at hand.

Mark turned to Murf. "Is there any chance that a move like this will cause Govern to investigate? If he moves any forces across the border, there will be trouble."

"He won't move an inch over the line without orders from me."

The two nobles were ushered into the guard room. In a few words Mark explained that he wanted of them. But as he talked he could see in their faces that the nobles had no intentions of complying.

"Your rule," he finished, "has been directed wholly by Erlayok. Here is a chance to do something useful on your own."

Erlaken laughed derisively. "We have been more or less ordered about by Erlayok, but our lands have been our own. You would place our wealth in the hands of the rabble. You'll get no help from us!"

"A misconception on your part," stated Mark. "When the new government is organized, your lands will still be your own. And you might even take useful parts in the management of that government, if your actions show you to be qualified. If we were so stupid as to kill off the better brains of the country, you would be dead now. But under the new government there will be no oppressive taxation, and no man will wield any power over the freedom of another man. High taxes won't be necessary, for a large army won't be needed. A fair income will be left you."

Erlahul sneered. "Armies won't be needed, eh? Shall we just send written invitations to our enemies?"

MARK'S FACE went grim. He saw futility of trying to convince these men. "I've no more time to waste," he said, turning to Smid. "These men have wives and children, haven't they?"

Smid nodded. The two nobles paled.

"There are some who think that all aristocrats should be exterminated," Mark said. "They can't seem to get it into their heads that you have countenanced the injustices meted out to them only because those things appeared to you to be the order of the day.

"They don't realize that such things have been entirely impersonal to you, and that you have never given any great thought to the matter. That you are really only guilty of laziness. They seem to think that you are malicious and cruel by nature, and that you won't change. They want revenge!

"I guess the best thing for me to do is to let *you* convince them that they're wrong, and wash my hands of the whole thing. Women are eloquent talkers. I'll see that your wives are given a chance to talk to these thick-headed ones, too."

Without further ado, the two nobles stepped forward and signed the orders.

Mark had them returned to the safety of their own castles. His bluff had worked.

Strangely, to both Murf and Smid, Mark burst into laughter. He had just remembered that he could have obtained the signatures instantly by means of hypnotism.

THE DAY dragged on endlessly, with no word from any of the other cities. A courier of Erlaken's retinue had been dispatched with the orders for the return of the nobles' armies. The man was known to the generals of the armies. These forces were the nearest to the City of Scarbor of all the armies of the lesser nobles, and Mark fervently hoped they would arrive before Erlayok's men.

There was a good chance that they would for although Erlayok's forces had a shorter distance to traverse, the country was rougher and the travel slower.

At the best there would be no sign of either army for three days.

Working almost continuously, the rebel leaders, with the valuable help of Jon, utilized the time in getting all the fighting men at hand ready to defend the city.

By the third day the city was as orderly and quiet as if no rebellion had taken place. More so, if anything, for there were no rowdy gangs of carousing soldiers on the streets.

Mark noticed in the faces of the people a certain quality which hadn't been there before. Heads were higher, and everywhere people seemed to feel freedom from fear. It wasn't generally known that there was still a good possibility that this freedom might be snatched from them at any minute.

Mark had thought it better that way, for if everything went all right the armies of Erlaken and Erlahul would arrive in time to protect the city from Erlayok's forces. If they didn't, no purpose would be served by getting the civilian population uneasy by telling them of the impending battle. Everything was being done for the defense of the city which could be done. There were dozens of outposts stationed along the routes by which both armies would approach.

In matters of civil government Jon showed his ability. The smooth, orderly way the city's normal operation was restored was due mainly to his efforts.

Murf and Smid quickly realized that Mark's choice of the Duke as the future supreme ruler of the Brish was a wise one.

He had been born to the job and was by far the most capable man for it.

During the morning of the third day dispatches arrived from the most distant of the cities informing them that the victory had gone to the rebels. Order had been restored and the rebel commanders were taking charge of all civil activities until such time as the permanent government took hold.

About noon of the third day, the blow fell.

A rider came into the prison courtyard, his horse covered with lather. He brought the news that Mark had been expecting. Less than ten miles outside of the city a large body of horsemen had been sighted coming from the north. They were estimated at about five hundred. But by their comparative slow pace it was believed that they were followed by a much larger body of men on foot.

No word was forthcoming from the route to the west, the direction from which their own forces would come.

"How many horses have we?" Mark inquired of Smid.

"A bare two hundred," was the answer. "But we can commandeer perhaps a thousand."

A hasty conference followed. It was planned to send only three hundred horsemen to engage the vanguard of Erlayok's forces. There was a thick wood to the west of the city at a distance of about two miles. The plan was for the rebel horsemen to engage the enemy briefly and then retreat, drawing them toward the forest. Previously placed in concealment would be as many archers as they could muster. These would pick off the enemy and capture as many horses as possible.

With the captured horses and the ones which could be commandeered, the rebels would be mounted and would be used against the main body of the enemy army. It was assumed, of course, that the enemy cavalry had all been sighted, and their total number was somewhere near five hundred.

It was a safe assumption, for it wasn't likely that any horsemen would be at the rear of the enemy forces. Their objective was directly before them and no flank was to be considered.

The big unknown factor in the rebels' plans was the number of foot soldiers they would have to fight.

CHAPTER XXIV

LONELY BATTLE

MARK RODE AT the head of the rebel cavalry. They approached the enemy from a tangent, slightly to the west of their line of march. Mark could see beyond the mounted force to the infantry behind it. And well to the rear he saw, bulking large in the midst of the walking soldiers, a horse and a rider. The animal was of tremendous proportion.

Even in the distance Mark could guess that it was a work horse pressed into service for an unusual purpose. On its back rode a huge man. Erlayok.

The rebel coup was carried out without a hitch. They engaged the enemy, and as Erlayok's cavalry began to execute a flanking move, by curling the ends of their formation into a crescent shape, Mark's horsemen retreated in what looked like a disorganized rout.

The enemy saw its chance to wipe out the inferior force, and followed at a gallop.

But when Mark's group reached the edge of the wood, it suddenly turned to give battle. And the archers got in their deadly work as the two bodies clashed.

Only a few escaped to return to the main body of Erlayok's army. And the horses taken were over three hundred.

At another conference between Mark, Jon, Murf and Smid, a plan for the next engagement was hastily worked out. Jon had taken part in the first brush, for the archers had been mainly his own men. But when the plans for the coming engagement were completed, he was surprised to find himself suddenly thrust into a cell.

To his indignant protests, Mark only grinned. Murf gave the key to the cell to Spud, with orders that if the enemy penetrated into the city to release the Duke and give him a chance to get his family to safety.

"You see," explained Mark. "One man won't make much difference out there. And it's going to be your job to run this country if we succeed in beating Erlayok. Men like you and Smid are not to be risked on the battlefield. You're too valuable."

They left him still protesting and went out to lead their forces, Mark with the cavalry and Murf with the infantry. They didn't delay, but put their plans into action at once. The further from the city the battle took place, the better.

Murf led his forces directly to the north, toward the center of Erlayok's main body. Mark remained out of sight with about twelve hundred horsemen, until the ground force was over half-way to the enemy.

The plan was to allow Erlayok's generals to observe that the opposing force was far inferior to their own. The obvious reaction would be to spread their men along a wide front, with the idea of flanking the smaller body.

It worked. But just before the two armies clashed and too late for the enemy to reform, Mark's cavalry dashed around the sides of Murf's force and plowed into the far-flung ends of enemy formation.

The maneuver was executed with such perfect timing that Erlayok's forces were thrown into confusion. Their superiority in numbers was quickly cut down. The compact central body of Murf's fighters, even though untrained and poorly equipped, cut the enemy forces in half.

Mark, in the thick of the battle, was dividing his attention between murderous use of his flashing axe, and keeping an eye on the whole engagement.

He looked ahead to the point where he had last seen the ponderous white horse of Erlayok's.

For a few minutes, the business of keeping enemy swords from hamstringing him kept him absorbed, and the next time he saw Erlayok, Erlayok was urging his mount to a gallop, in full retreat. Mark glanced ahead of him. There, coming at a trot, was a large body of foot-soldiers.

Mark ordered a retreat, on the double.

The rebel cavalry allowed Murf's group to retire first, covering their retreat. But the shattered forces of the enemy made no attempt to pursue. They reformed and waited for the new arrivals to come up.

It would have been folly to attempt to fight any longer out in the open. They were outnumbered two to one. The only hope now lay in keeping the enemy from entering the city. If they could hold Erlayok off until the armies of the other earls arrived, victory was certain.

Mark was assailed by a sudden fear when he thought of this. It was possible that something had happened to Erlaken's courier, and no armies would arrive! He had thought of sending several men for that job, but had hated to take any of his fighters away at a time when it appeared he would need every man.

Fortunately the City of Scarbor was not a scraggly affair with its houses thinning toward its outer edges. It had been built obviously for defense. Its edges were clearly defined and not jutting out haphazardly. The last house on each street came opposite the last house on the adjoining street.

Quite a few of the streets ended in high walls, joining the houses. There were only about thirty streets in the whole city which were not thus protected. Roads led out from these to the surrounding countryside.

Mark and Murf worked like Trojans, deploying their forces where they would do the most good. Jon's archers and as many of the rebels who could handle a bow were stationed on the rooftops. The rest were placed at the street entrances.

Chains were hastily stretched across between the buildings.

As Erlayok's formidable force approached it split into a dozen sections. Lacking siege equipment none attempted to assail the walls, but each body stormed the street entrance nearest to it.

Time after time the defenders beat them back. And time after time reïnforcements were rushed to some street where too many deaths had weakened the defense.

MARK KEPT moving from point to point, lending his deadly axe when he spotted places which were weakening. The battle waged for an hour, the invaders not gaining an inch. But the victory was going to Erlayok just the same.

Although his forces were suffering heavily, the dead beginning to pile up at the chained street entrances, the defenders were dying also, though in lesser numbers.

But while Erlayok was holding men in reserve to fill the places of the fallen, Mark's numbers were strictly limited. Already he was having trouble keeping all the points of assault covered with sufficient men to hold them.

As his no-longer-gleaming axe became slippery with the red creeping up its handle, Mark's thoughts wandered away from the hopeless battle.

He still shouted meaningless encouragement to the desperate rebels, but fighting had become a mechanical thing. His tireless body and lightning, reflexes protected him from too dangerous wounds. And it wasn't necessary for him to devote his undivided attention to the business of fighting. His thoughts strayed. Strayed to the one he would probably never see again. Nona.

There was no hope in him any more. The end of his adventure was too clearly discernible in the way the fight was progressing. And as long as these courageous farmers and laborers continued to mock their fate, he knew that he would stay to the end.

And the end would be his end. Erlayok would see to that. The mad noble would carve his body into so many bits that not even a jig-saw puzzle expert would be able to put them together again.

The vision of the lovely Nona danced before him. He saw her now as he used to see her during those mock battles aboard the Viking ship. He smiled as he watched her determined expression, the flowing grace of her beautiful body, the flashing sweeps of the double-bitted axe in her hand....

CHAPTER XXV

FAIR HARBOR

A LONE FIGURE stood atop the little knoll and gazed toward the west. Eyes shaded from a sun that was low on the horizon, she seemed to be searching, perplexedly. A little while before she had seen a terrific battle in progress at the very place she was now inspecting.

She had been on board a vessel, coming toward the shore, when she had sighted the conflict. A rise of land had hidden it from her as the ship approached a landing. When her vessel had beached she had dashed ashore ahead of her shipmates and climbed to the top of the rise.

But in the interval the battle had finished and none but the dead and dying remained to mark the spot.

She looked beyond the site of the conflict and wondered if the men had vanished into the thick wood she saw there.

Then she turned and saw that all four of the ships of her fleet had beached, and pouring from them were hundreds of huge Viking rovers, all armed with axe and shortsword. These were the fighters she had brought with her, the breed who would rather fight than eat and whose appetites were tremendous.

Proudly she watched them swarm across the beach. They were all men who had rallied at her call, wanting nothing but the opportunity to lay down their lives for her and for her man, Mark. They had even been told that Mark would disapprove of looting in this country, but had come just the same.

As she watched them there came to her sensitive ears faint sounds, shouting, cries of pain, carried on a vagrant breeze. She turned her head, trying to locate the source.

Her eyes chanced on a city in the distance. In landing she had seen this city, but in her anxiety to see if her man was engaged in the battle on the plain, she had forgotten it. But now, looking more fixedly, she saw tiny groups moving toward the dark rectangles formed by gaps between the flat sides of houses and walls. Gaps which were street ends.

Still watching, she saw an occasional tiny flash of light within the shadowed recesses of these rectangles. Flashes such as might be made by stray beams of sunlight reflected on axe and sword-blades.

Suddenly she sprang into action, leaping down from the knoll and running toward her Vikings. In seconds she had the entire band in motion, trotting toward the city.

She sped along before them, not taking her eyes from the scene at its edge.

Getting closer by the minute she made out more and more detail. Occasionally she would get a glimpse of a dented helmet adorned with wings, moving about among the defenders. Then she would lose sight of it, only to see it reappear a hundred yards away, at another of the street entrances.

She led her band directly toward the place where the greatest number of the invaders seemed to be concentrated, for it was there that the winged helmet appeared the more often.

With a wordless roar which had been heard in ancient Copenhagen, the Vikings plowed into the besiegers. Veterans of a dozen battles, every man of them, they made quick inroads into the mass of Erlayok's men.

AT THE deafening sound of the Norsemen's battle cry and the clashing of axes which immediately followed, Erlayok wheeled his ponderous mount and urged it to a clumsy gallop. He had been directing the attack on the city at a safe distance from the fighting. But now he suddenly found himself in the thick of it.

The Vikings were boring through his reserves and he was directly in their path!

Frantically he dug his heels into the flanks of his mount, at the same time flaying it with the reins. His one driving impulse was to leave the vicinity with all haste. This battle was already lost, he could see. His men would never be able to stand before these giant Norsemen.

But if he could get clear, there were many thousands of soldiers who could yet be rallied in a second attempt to retake the city. This time he would drag every regiment he could muster from the borders.

He should have done that in the first place, he realized now. But he had been confident that a few thousand soldiers would be sufficient to beat back the poorly equipped rebels and he had returned with the first few regiments he had contacted.

The draft horse he was riding was doing its best to obey his frantic urging and seemed to be getting every last bit of speed out of its ponderous body. The Vikings were pressing nearer, driving through the ranks of Erlayok's men with little effort.

Actually their advance was far too slow to cut off the flight of the Earl, but to him it seemed that they would be upon him in a few seconds. His horse was thundering away parallel to their advance, and was almost clear when he again flayed at its shoulders with the ends of the rein.

It was a fatal mistake.

One end of the rein flicked momentarily at the horse's eyes as he made to strike again. At the sudden pain the horse faltered in its stride and reared, throwing off the Earl. He fell heavily, but was on his feet immediately.

Gone now was all thought of flight. He couldn't get clear if he tried. And with the knowledge he determined to take as many Vikings as possible before one of them got him. But even in this resolve he was thwarted.

His sword was barely clear of its scabbard when a brawny Norseman gleefully cut at him with a battle-axe. The cut landed, cleaving through his helmet as if it were tissue paper, Erlayok went down without striking a blow.

Nona, her axe weaving and slashing with equal effect to that of the brawniest of her Norsemen, fought her way toward the spot where she could see the dented headpiece of her husband rising a foot above the head-level of the men he was battling.

As her flashing axe and darting shortsword cleared a path for her she saw his face, grim and sad. He was fighting with the mechanical precision and efficiency of a machine, but by his face his thoughts were far away.

Then his eyes seemed to light on her, as she fought her way closer to him.

She saw the smile that was at once happy and sad, but he still seemed to be moving and seeing in a dream. His axe sheared the arm from one of the invaders, and moved sideways to sink in the neck of another. His body weaved to avoid the lunge of a striking sword and he back-stepped to allow a battle-axe whistle harmlessly past—but the expression remained the same through it all.

THEN IT changed—and Nona found herself fighting for her life. She had forged too far into that mass of fighting maniacs. The enemy was on both sides of her as well as to the front. Her body weaved and dodged with desperate rapidity. Her axe slashed and bit deeply. Her sword wove a gleaming wall around her.

But in spite of it she felt the bite of a dagger in the flesh of an arm, and a hammering blow on her helmet. Time after time momentary flashes of pain marked the slice or stab of an enemy weapon.

Wildly her lips formed the word, "Mark!" And with a roar which drowned out all other sound, a fighting avalanche of furious bone and muscle dove at the enemy surrounding her.

They melted in the savagery of the onslaught. In an instant she was gathered in capable arms and raised aloft, carried back away from the din of the fighting.

For a long minute Mark crushed her to him, then released

her to hold her at arm's length. He feasted his eyes for another long silent minute, then frowned.

"Nona—you crazy, wonderful lunatic! Where on earth did you come from?"

She smoothed down an almost non-existent dress and patted his cheek before replying. Her expression was elaborately casual, though her eyes did give her away.

"I knew you'd get in trouble if you were left alone," she said. "So I gathered some of the boys to help out. You're so helpless, you know, that…" She couldn't continue, for her lips had suddenly become very, very busy.

LESS THAN a month later the four Viking ships were being provisioned for the return voyage to Stadtland. The Norsemen were well satisfied with the results of their little venture. True, they had wanted nothing, but the trip had been profitable nevertheless.

They had been feted in half a dozen cities, and loaded with presents in each. The people of this land had suddenly found that they were in a position to be generous for favors received. The coffers of certain of the nobles who had fought to the last ditch, and whose property had been confiscated as a result, contained wealth in abundance.

Erlayok's riches alone would have paid for all the damage done in the rebellion.

Furthermore the Brish had found that there was no more need for the swollen armies they had been supporting, and their taxes were going to drop as a result.

Word had gone to the kingdoms to the north and the west, and a permanent peace had been established. Thousands of men were coming from the armies to enter industry of all kinds, and places were being found for them.

And the taxes which were necessary would be borne by a greater number. There would be a long period of industrial reorganization before everything would run smoothly, but during that period no man or woman would suffer. There were vast hoarded sums to carry the government through this period. More than would be needed.

Jon was carrying on, with the enthusiastic cooperation of everyone, as the new king. Smid was elevated to dukedom, and was working as he had always worked, for the betterment of his people. Murf, now admittedly the Mic that he was, remained as the ambassador of his father.

A new era had begun, and Mark's work was done. At the rail of the flagship as it left the shores of the land of the Brish, Nona looked up and read an uneasiness in his eyes.

"Now, Mark, when you get that look in your eyes. Oh well, I suppose there's no sense in arguing. More worlds to conquer?"

"Perhaps," he said, loftily. Then he smiled. "No, that isn't it. I've forgotten something, but I don't know what it is."

With a derisive tilt to her eyebrows she surveyed his single garment, and the belt from which hung his axe and a dagger.

"You didn't have much to start with, if I remember correctly," she observed.

"No," he pondered. "It wasn't anything like that. I believe it's something I forgot to do. Oh never mind, I'll think of it some-time."

As he said this, they suddenly noticed a strange contrivance, on the deck beside them, which hadn't been there a minute before. It was a table-like affair of spools, wheels, needle and thread. A treadle situated between its feet was oscillating merrily away without visible, means of locomotion. Nona raised a hand to her lips.

"Whatever is that?" she asked through her fingers.

"A sewing machine," said Mark, resignedly.

At these words, the contrivance vanished and was replaced by a fearsome monstrosity which clanked, snorted and rattled. It was quite large and formidable appearing. Nona's eyes asked the question.

"A threshing machine," Mark explained.

There followed a bewildering procession of machines

designed for every purpose imaginable, and most of them noisy and awe-inspiring. Nona was beginning to become a bit upset. There came a lull in the squeaking and clattering—an electric fan was humming softly and blowing Nona's hair at the moment—and Mark explained.

"THIS," HE said, "is Omega's gentle reminder that I practically blackmailed him into stealing the designs of a certain machine. After which I promptly forgot all about it, and didn't even stick around to see if he succeeded. Very ill-mannered of me, and he's letting me know what he thinks about it."

Abruptly the fan disappeared and Omega revealed himself in his usual caricature of an old man, toothless and decrepit.

"I'll accept that as an apology," he said, crisply. "It's all I'm likely to get. And of course, not so much as a word of thanks."

"Things were sort of hectic," Mark said. "What with the revolution breaking out just after I talked to you." His apologetic expression suddenly left as he thought of the lion he had been confronted with at Omega's departure on that occasion. "Say at that maybe it's you who owe me an apology. You're as absent-minded as I am. That lion might have bitten an arm off me, when you decided to leave."

Omega chuckled. "I did that for revenge," he said. "But of course if he had managed to dispose of your arm I'd have given you a new one."

"Thanks. Well, we're even then. Where's the machine?"

"You don't need it, do you?"

Mark hesitated. "No, not exactly, though it might come in handy some time. I could drive a ship with it, you know."

"Nothing doing! The race which invented it not only drove ships with it, they did everything with it which required power. And once they had bent it to every purpose it could fulfill, they sat back and enjoyed the fruits of their work. They had a perfect mechanical civilization! Everything they could possibly desire was provided for them.

"But when the time came that their sun was approaching the

point where it was about to burst, none of them had intelligence enough to move their planet out of harm's way. Yet they could have done that little thing if they had still possessed the knowledge that was theirs at the time of its invention."

Mark got it. "You mean that once they had achieved perfection, they let up?"

"Precisely," Omega affirmed. "They ceased to improve their minds and those minds stagnated. They had built a machine which usurped a function of their brains. That function still remains to be developed in your own brain, as well as the one which would give you control of telepathy, and you will have to develop them yourself.

"I'm not going to give you that machine! Given time, of which you have plenty, you should be able to master the function which will give you control over the forces of nature. You will learn to transport yourself, by mental action, anywhere you wish. You might even learn to create matter from energy. Crudely, of course. In your lifetime you'll never be able to learn how to construct living bodies or even good copies. Your descendants will, though. But they never would if I gave you this machine."

Mark grinned. "All right," he soothed. "Don't get all het up about it. I don't need the machine anyway."

"So I found out after I came back from my travel in time. I dropped in on some of the leaders of the Mics and the Macs. All they wanted was peace and normal commerce between their respective countries and the Brish. The whole thing was an unnatural condition brought about by the lust for power in Erlayok.

"On one of my visits I overheard a conversation which told me of the status of Murf. So instead of coming back with the machine which you thought you needed, I decided to give you a chance to get things straight. Your horse was very surprised when I forced him to make that turn."

"You did that?" Mark exclaimed. "Why didn't you let me

know you were there? You could have given me the whole story and saved a lot of time."

Omega chuckled. "Murf had no trouble convincing you. And besides, I prefer to watch things develop in a more normal manner. I don't like to go about confounding people."

"No, of course not," said Mark.

"Well, we've got that settled," Omega said. "I'll see you again sometime. So long!"

"So long!"

For sometime after Omega had made his usual abrupt departure, Mark and Nona, arms entwined, gazed out over the endless vista of the swelling sea. In Nona's eyes was an expression of supreme content and happiness. In Mark's, there was at first the dancing gleam which reflected his innate spirit of unrest. But as the soothing influence of the swelling billows penetrated, and he became conscious of Nona's cool, firm flesh hollowed in the crook of his arm, his eyes also reflected the serenity and content which was hers.

THE ARGOSY LIBRARY ™

SERIES 7 INCLUDES:

* BRAND * TUTTLE * BECHDOLT *

HORN * MCCULLEY * ROSCOE *

* HALL & FLINT *

* BEYER * MCCALL *

* MONTGOMERY *

THE BEST FICTION
FROM THE FRANK
A. MUNSEY LINE